Letters From the Heart

S.L. STERLING

Peggy

I knelt on the ground, brushing some of the dead, dry leaves from the tombstone at my late husband's grave, his name coming into view. Darren Hollis 1984-2015. A tear escaped my eye.

"I'm sorry I haven't been here in a while," I said quietly. "I don't want to say I've been too busy, but I've been busy. Peggy's Petals has really taken off. I've been so busy with orders that I've had to hire not only a delivery driver, but a couple students to help." I smiled, looking down at his name. "I think you'd be proud."

I placed the small arrangement of 'Stargazer' lilies beside his name and placed my gardening pillow on the ground, sitting myself on it. I hadn't been to his graveside for a while, but I'd had to drive into Cedar's Landing to get some supplies for the shop. It was the first day it wasn't raining, so I figured it was a good day to come. Letting out a sigh, I stared at his name.

"As much as I worried that moving to Willow Valley would be a bad thing, it turned out to be an excellent decision. I have so many things I want to tell you. The most important being that I wish you were still here. Life has been interesting without you."

I looked down at the grass in front of me and watched as a ladybug made her way up onto a blade of grass. I placed my hand down and allowed the little red bug to crawl into my hand.

"Darren, it's been lonely navigating all these waters alone. All these unknown territories. The house needs a lot of repair and renovation work. You can only imagine how much I don't know about that stuff. I know you'd love Willow Valley, and most times, I still feel that you are there with me. Sometimes, I still catch the scent of your cologne and think to myself, you must be right behind me. I've even caught myself talking to you as if you were in the room," I murmured, watching the little red bug make its way over my fingers.

"Anyway, the store is doing well, and I love Willow Valley. One of the local girls who works at The Crispy Biscuit, Melinda, just started an army pen pal program. Her father is a marine, and I guess he just got re-deployed, so she feels this is the perfect time. Trinity wants me to join her in writing letters." I swallowed hard. "She says it will be more fun if we both do it." I rolled my eyes thinking back to our conversation over coffee the other morning.

"You know, Darren, I can barely remember what your voice sounds like. With every day that passes, another part of you floats away from me. I can't feel your touch anymore. When you first were gone, I could lie in bed and close my eyes and still feel you beside me, your arms around me, but now that is gone. It scares me. I'm afraid that one day I am going to wake up and all I'm going to have left to remember you by is a name and a date." I wiped at the tears that escaped my eyes. "And the horrible memory of never being able to apologize to you for all those things I said, to tell you I love you before you left me." Tears slid down my cheeks as I thought back to that night.

"It seems people think I should start dating again. I keep telling them I'm not ready, but really, it's more that I'm afraid of what you might think. I know that sounds silly, since you aren't here anymore, but we never talked about what would happen if one of us were no longer here. However, I also didn't think that conversation was important because I didn't plan on being a widow before we got a chance to really begin our life together, either. If I think about it, I'm sure you're probably up there rolling your eyes at me, thinking I'm being ridiculous. I can almost hear you laugh at me."

Growing quiet, I looked out at the small pond in the cemetery. I'd picked this spot for Darren, right at the edge of the pond, because he'd loved to fish. It was his happy place on weekends. I'd figured this would be the best final resting spot for my husband. "It's been almost eight years since you left me. For whatever reason, I'm finding this year to be harder than the rest. Well, perhaps not harder than the first, but... this year is harder." I swallowed hard, forcing the guilt from my mind.

As I looked out over the small body of water, a Trumpeter swan landed and began swimming toward me. Confused at the fact the bird was alone, I watched him for a while. I remembered the first time I'd ever seen one. Darren and I had gone out to a lake to fish, and two had landed on the water. At first, because of their size, I was afraid of them, and as they swam closer to the boat, Darren wrapped his arms around me and pulled me into him, holding me tight.

"No need to be afraid, Peggy," he'd said. "Him and his girl are just out on a date like us." He kissed my cheek.

I smiled and watched the two large birds swim around the water. "Or I wonder if that is his flavor of the month." I giggled.

Darren chuckled. "Actually, Trumpeter swans, they mate for life."

"Really."

"Yep. I've even heard that if one mate dies, sometimes the one left behind never mates again. It's rare but happens."

"Wow, can you imagine, only ever having one mate?" I giggled.

"Do I need to be worried about you?" Darren asked, tickling my side.

I laughed. "Watch it, mister. You never know what sort of harem I may have waiting. You know, I do have all those men in my romance novels." I giggled.

"To think, all my friends warned me about you." He winked. "They told me not to trust the quiet ones, especially the ones that read romance books, and yet here I am, with the quietest one of the bunch."

The sound of wings fluttering caused me to jump, and I watched as the swan climbed up on the grass just a few feet away from me. He waddled along, picking at the grass, and then stopped and looked directly at me. He stood there, watching me for what seemed forever, and then something scared him, and he spread his wings and took off in the opposite direction.

"Darren, did you see that?" I whispered to the emptiness, just as I'd been doing all afternoon.

I smiled as I watched the swan fly off. I looked down

at the stone that held my late husband's name and wondered what we might have had had he still been here.

"I guess I'll see you in a few months, when I come back to Cedar Landing for more supplies. Just know that I miss you. Just know I'd be here more often if I could be."

I flipped the sign on the front door to closed and turned the little lock. Checking the time, I noticed I was already late. My last customer had come in to place an order and didn't have the slightest clue what she wanted. Rushing around the shop, I put the last of the flowers that were still out back into the cooler and then grabbed my purse and made my way out the back door.

I had ten minutes to get down to Bluebird Books to meet Trinity. We'd promised Melinda and Brooke we'd be at The Crispy Biscuit for the announcement of this new pen pal program. I glanced at my watch again and picked up my pace and arrived just as Trinity was locking up the store.

"Hey, lady!" I waved as I crossed the street. "Sorry I'm late."

"Hey! I was getting worried that you wouldn't make it

on time." Trinity pulled her key from the door of the store and shoved it in her purse before giving me a hug.

"I knew I should have locked up early." I glanced around. "Where's Thomas? Isn't he joining us as well?"

"Unfortunately, not. He had to go pick up some lumber just outside of town for a project he's been working on. He said, if he is back in time, that he'd join us, but I think it's safe to say it will just be the two of us."

"That's too bad. I know Melinda was looking forward to having us all there to support her with the start of this new program."

"I know. Thomas felt bad. He too was hoping to go, but he's been waiting for this order for a few weeks now."

"That's understandable. He probably doesn't want to disappoint his customer either."

"That's just it. The customer has been waiting for a while now. How was work today? Were you busy?"

"Oh gosh, you should have been at the store today." I whispered, "So many people, but my favorite was this young guy. He was about fifteen years old. He was all nervous and jittery. His face went red when he told me he wanted to buy flowers for his new girlfriend. It was so sweet."

"Ah, young love," Trinity said. "I remember those days."

"Yes, young love," I repeated.

Trinity bumped her shoulder into mine. "You know,

Peggy, you aren't too old for young love." Trinity looked at me. "I mean, look at Thomas and I. Or Vi and Jed."

I couldn't help but laugh. "Please, your stories are ones we only read about in romance novels. You know, the only section I live in at your store." I giggled. "They don't really happen to the everyday average person."

"Oh, Peggy, don't doubt Cupid's arrow. These stories happen every day to people. Where else do you think authors get the inspiration to write them?"

"From their imaginations," I said, pointing to my head.

"Come on, no one's imagination is that good."

"Okay, then tell me, who was the last person you knew who met a billionaire in the streets, struck up a fake relationship with them, and ended up with a happily ever after?"

Trinity thought for a moment and then broke out into laughter. "I don't know. I don't think I know any billionaires."

"Exactly!" We both laughed as we continued walking down the road.

We picked up to a brisk pace as we made our way toward The Crispy Biscuit, the warm spring air growing a little cooler now that the sun was setting.

"So, are you going to actually write a letter?" I questioned.

"I think so. I think Melinda has a great idea. These

men and women are far from their families, and when I was speaking with Melinda, she told me that a lot of them don't have family to write home to. I think if we can make a difference in someone's life than we should do it."

"Yeah, that is rather sad, isn't it? Off fighting for their country or keeping the peace in another one and not having someone to talk to, to support them. That also means that they don't have something to look forward to. A simple letter from a friend could make an enormous difference."

"What about you? You going to write one?" Trinity asked. I could feel her stare burning into me as she waited for my response.

"I don't know." I shrugged. "What would I say?"

Trinity thought for a moment, "Well, I'd start by just writing a letter. Tell them a bit about yourself. You know, just like you would if you were on a blind date."

"Oh, lord!" I giggled. "Do we know who we are writing to, or is it exactly that. A blind date letter? Sort of like being in a chat room on the internet?"

Trinity did her best to keep a straight face. "When I spoke to Melinda, she said that the program pairs you up with someone. I'm not sure if they read the letters or if they just randomly hand them out to someone. To be honest, I think it's sort of exciting."

We stopped in front of The Crispy Biscuit and looked inside. The seats were full, and I could see Brooke and

Tristan prepping a tray of drinks behind the counter. "Well, I guess I can think about writing the letter." I shrugged. "I'll make my decision after the meeting."

"Oh, Peggy, come on, you need to do this. Melinda is counting on our support."

"I don't know. It would be easier for me if we knew who we were writing to."

Trinity waved her hand in front of her face, dismissing what I'd said. "Nonsense. Not knowing is half the fun. Come on, let's go in and find out what it's all about, and we will go from there."

"Whatever you say."

"Come on. Live a little. Get excited. We will have a letter writing party. It will be fun," Trinity said as she pulled the door open. We stepped inside, nodded to Brooke and Tristan, and then took a seat at our usual table.

I pulled the door open to Bluebird Books and stepped inside. Trinity was focused on whatever it was she was working on. She finally glanced up from the counter and put her pencil down.

"Hey," she greeted.

"Hey. How's things?" I said, making my way over to where she stood.

It wasn't normal for me to show up in the middle of the afternoon, but I didn't have a choice today. After the meeting, Trinity twisted my arm and got me to agree to write at least one letter. Melinda would be collecting them today and getting ready to send off the first batch.

"Great, it's been busy today. This is the first downtime I've had. Now tell me, did you write that letter? Or are we both heading down to The Crispy Biscuit to only hand one in?"

I pressed my lips together. "Well, I wrote one, but I don't know if it's good enough to send. I should have had you write it for me." I shrugged.

"Oh gosh, just let me see it?" Trinity held out her hand, waiting.

I met her eyes, trying to decide if I should let her read it. She didn't back down. Instead, she looked right into my eyes, her hand still out, waiting.

"I'm waiting."

With a sigh, I reached into my purse and pulled out the envelope that contained the letter I'd written. I knew I should have sealed the envelope instead of leaving it open. Feeling like it wasn't good enough, I took a deep breath and then placed it in Trinity's hand. "Don't you dare laugh," I warned.

"Peggy, why would I laugh?" Trinity said, beginning to giggle already.

"See, you're laughing already, and you haven't even read it yet."

"Oh stop. I am not. I'm laughing at you."

I even stifled a giggle at the situation myself. "I'll be over—"

"Over in the 'these things don't happen to the ordinary person' section?"

"You got it. Going to find me a new book boyfriend. One that will sweep me off my feet." I laughed and walked over to the romance area, pulling a couple of books from the shelf. I looked at the cover and then sat down to look them over while Trinity opened my letter.

As she read the letter, I kept glancing over at her, waiting to see if there was any type of reaction on her face, but she kept the same peaceful look the entire time. When she finished, she shoved the letter back inside the envelope and placed it on the counter, not saying anything. I couldn't wait any longer. I jumped up off the chair, leaving the books I'd been looking at on the chair, and went over to her. "Well?"

"Well, it's good, Peggy. You'd be silly not to send it. You are going to make a difference to someone, and that alone should make you want to send it. This is a really great program."

"I know this program is a good thing. I guess I'm just apprehensive." I shrugged.

"Oh goodness! Why?" Trinity asked, pouring me a coffee.

I thought for a moment, trying to put into words how I felt, hoping that Trinity would understand. "Promise me you won't laugh?"

Trinity nodded and placed a full mug of hot coffee down in front of me, waiting for me to explain my reasoning. I looked around at the shelves of books. You'd have thought that the characters on the pages were listening. I swallowed hard, leaned forward, and whispered, "I guess I'm afraid that they might pair me with a man."

Trinity smiled softly to herself, but she didn't laugh. Instead, a look of understanding crossed her face. She'd known that I was coming up on the eighth anniversary of Darren's death. She also knew I was having a considerably harder time this year than the first year he'd been gone and that I'd not dated since.

"I don't think you have anything to worry about."

"Yeah, but what if one day the person wants to meet?"

"Oh, my dear, don't be silly. We aren't playing matchmaker here. This is strictly to keep these men and women company while they are gone from their friends and family. However, from the other side of things, what would be so wrong with meeting someone?"

I looked at her, certain that a look of horror was written on my face. "What would be wrong with it?"

"Yeah, I mean, say it is a man. You write back and forth, share stories, really get to know someone. What on earth would be wrong with meeting that person? Who the hell knows, he may even come with a completely sculpted chest, and abs, and that amazingly carved V all of us romance readers swoon about." She winked.

Trinity knew me way too well. She knew exactly what to say to get me going. I felt my cheeks heat. "You are baffling. You know exactly what to say, don't you. I guess nothing would be wrong with meeting someone." I shrugged. "Except the fact I'm not sure I'm ready for that."

Trinity laughed. "Well, I don't think we need to worry about you meeting someone from the first letter." She giggled, handing me my envelope back. "Besides, until we get a response, we won't have a clue who will be reading the letter we wrote. We also don't even know if they will write back, so I think for now you're safe."

Just then, the bells above the door jingled, and we both turned to see Ava walk in, her book bag slung over her shoulder, book in her hand.

"Hey, Ava," we both said in unison.

Tearing her eyes off the page, she looked up. "Hey, Trinity. Mrs. Hollis. Sorry I'm a few minutes late. I was waiting for my teacher to hand out our assignments.

Then I started reading this book, and well…you know what happens. You won't be late because of me, will you?"

"No, dear, the meeting at The Crispy Biscuit is for five. We have lots of time to get there," Trinity said, meeting my eyes as she handed me my letter. "Grab yourself a drink from the fridge in the back and a muffin off the table. We will head out shortly."

As soon as Ava was settled, we made our way down to The Crispy Biscuit. Melinda was behind the counter serving a customer and greeted us both with a smile as we stepped inside. "Hey, ladies." She waved.

"Hey, Melinda. We are here with our letters," Trinity replied. "Wanted to make sure we got them in to you in time."

"Oh great! Give me a minute and let me grab the basket."

Once Melinda returned, Trinity and she began talking while I searched the display case for some type of sweet treat for after dinner. I listened with half an ear as Melinda spoke more about the program and how her best friend had just gotten married to her military pen pal. A funny feeling came over me as I stood there pretending to still search for a sweet treat to order, the letter still tucked into my purse.

"Oh, that is wonderful, Melinda. Is this the friend who lives outside of Willow Valley?"

"Yes. The one I mentioned the other night. They just left on their honeymoon this morning."

Brooke appeared from the kitchen and began joining in the conversation, followed by Tristan. As they all stood there talking, I pulled my letter from my purse and looked down at the white envelope. Still unsure that it was good enough, I looked at my small group of friends and made sure they weren't looking, then silently placed it in the trash just below where the basket sat. I jumped when I heard Trinity call my name.

"Huh, what?" I asked, looking up to see my best friend watching me.

"I said, did you put your letter in the box?"

"Yep." I swallowed hard. "Can I get some of these cookies to go, please?" I pointed to the new M&M's cookies in the display case. I needed to divert her attention off this damn letter.

Immediately, Tristan stepped in and began placing some cookies into a box for me. "Here you go, Peggy," he said, passing the box over the counter. "They are to die for, if I do say so myself."

"He's only saying that because he created the recipe," Brooke said, coming up behind him, wrapping her arms around his waist.

"We really should get going," I said, turning to Trinity.

"Yeah, true. I need to get home and get dinner before

Thomas returns. "Peggy, will you be joining us tonight?" she questioned.

"No, I still have some things to do at the shop. You can take some cookies for dessert, though," I said, holding the box out for her to take. "I'm just going to use the washroom before we go." Flashing what I was certain was a normal smile, and hoping Trinity hadn't seen where I'd put my letter, I crossed the restaurant and ducked into the washroom.

Ethan

One month later

It was Sunday night. I'd just showered after having returned from dinner. Lying down on my cot, I adjusted the pillow behind my head and reached for the phone. I looked forward to this time every month. It was one of relaxation, if only for a day, that I didn't have to worry about my men and could spend my time talking with my daughter. I dialed Melinda's number carefully, looking down at my small notebook to make sure I hadn't made a mistake, and waited while the call finally connected.

"Hello," I heard her voice come over the phone.

It had been a long time since I'd seen my daughter—years. I'd needed an out after her mother died. So, I used the military. It kept me busy, and at the time, it was what I wanted, but now I knew it hadn't been kind to family life and I missed her. "Hey, sweetie. It's your dad."

"Hey, Dad. How are you?"

"Doing okay. What about you?"

"Doing good. You'll be happy to know that things are going well for me here."

It had been fifteen years since her mother died. Soon after her funeral, I'd left for a peacekeeping mission, and I'd left Melinda behind to live with her aunt and uncle. I felt they could give her a more stable life than I could. I'd been right. They raised her in a loving home, treated her as if she were their own, while I moved from mission to mission. I sent money to support her and called as often as I could, and at least I knew she had what I wasn't able to give. Looking back on the situation, I was the absentee father she needed during that time, and as of late, I felt I needed to make that up to her.

"Glad to hear it. You still working at that bakery?" I asked. When Melinda finished school, she left our hometown and settled in Willow Valley.

"The Crispy Biscuit, yes. I love it there. They've given me more responsibility there, too, since Christmas. I really stepped up when Brooke got hurt."

"That's good. How is Willow Valley?"

"Honestly, I love it here. I know you'd love it there too, Dad." She paused, as if waiting for me to respond, but when I didn't, she cleared her throat and continued, "Oh, did you get my letter?"

I glanced over at my side table. I had gotten her last letter; it still lay on the top of the pile of my mail. "Yes, I did."

"Well, what do you think? I expected a response. Did you want to take part in that program I'm organizing?"

She'd written to me to tell me about an army pen pal program she was starting. I was proud of my girl that she'd started something like this. Some of my men received very few letters from their families. Some were completely alone, and I'd seen the effects that had on them. That was why, when Melinda originally brought it up to me, I said that my crew would love to take part. I'd had each of my men, who wished to take part, give me their names, and I'd sent them to her. However, I'd failed to put my name down.

"It surprised me to see that your name wasn't on the list, Dad. Did you not want to take part? I know you only have a year left and then you're retiring, but it's still a year, Dad. A year of being alone. A year of only receiving my letters, which I'm sure they aren't that great." She giggled. "I mean, how much do you really want to know about baking?"

I let out a breath. "Don't kid yourself. I love hearing from you, kid. I want to hear all about baking. In fact, I want to hear everything about you and your life. Yes, you are correct, I have one more year left. I just don't know what I am going to do after I leave here."

"Well, Dad, it's still a year. I hoped that you'd come and join me in Willow Valley when you retire. It would be nice to get to spend time with you again. I really think you'd like it here. It's quiet, and there are a few military men that have settled here."

"I know. You've told me before."

The line grew quiet. Then I heard Melinda clear her throat. "Dad, can I ask you something?"

"Of course, you can."

"How come you never remarried?"

I looked over at the small side table and at the small pictures of my wife and daughter. The most recent picture I'd received of Melinda had stopped me in my tracks. She was the spitting image of her mother. It was almost as if I were looking at a picture of my late wife when she was Melinda's age. I won't lie. It tugged at my heart.

"My dear, I hope you never understand my reasonings. What I will say is that work took over, and I needed to invest my time here." It wasn't a lie; it was the truth. Sort of. I'd buried myself in my job, pledging myself to my men instead of finding a life for myself, and that allowed me to protect my heart. It wasn't much of a life, anyway, always being away from the ones you loved. I'd realized that after Polly had died and you would have thought I'd want to be with my daughter, but somehow, being here was what eventually healed me.

"What are you going to do when you retire? You're going to need people, Dad."

She was right. I would need people. As she'd suggested, I was seriously considering moving to Willow Valley. I just needed to make sure that move was the right one for me before I said anything to her. "I know, Melinda, and as I told you, I would think about it."

"I'm glad to hear it. Now, with that said, this would be the best time then to agree to join the army pen pal program." I could hear the laughter in her voice. How did I not see that coming?

I let out a deep breath. "All right, you win. I feel like I was just ambushed." I laughed.

"You kinda were, and honestly, I figured you would have seen that coming from a mile away. Perhaps you are losing your touch!" She giggled.

"Hey now, I'll have you know I am still as sharp as I was years ago."

I watched as Sanders carried a large mailbag over his shoulder and dropped it down on the floor. "Mail call!" he shouted as he dug into the bag.

Moments later, I was sitting down sifting through my small pile of mail when a blank envelope caught my eye. The only giveaway was a sticker on the back sealing it shut that read APP. I smiled. While I wasn't keen on developing a friendship with a stranger, I still tore open the letter. Unfolding the letter, I straightened out the pages and sat back in my chair and started reading.

> To a new friend,
> I really do not know what to write. So, I'll start by saying my best friend, Trinity, coerced me into participating in this program. She keeps telling me I need to meet new people. I think secretly she just wants me to meet a man so I can date. The entire thought scares the daylights out of me. You see, I lost my husband a few years ago, eight to be exact, which I realize is a very personal fact about me, especially to write in a letter to someone I don't know.
> Anyway, let me introduce myself. My name is Peggy Hollis. I live in the small town of Willow Valley. It's a cute little town, and one

I'm thrilled to call home. I haven't always lived here. I moved here, yes, after he passed away. I never thought I'd find a place to call home again, but I did. The residents opened their hearts and doors to me quickly, as we all do when someone new comes to town. That is how I met my best friend, Trinity. She owns a small bookstore, Bluebird Books. I am a reader of romance, and once I'd settled, I found I needed something to pass the evenings away. I was in luck because her store has a great romance section.

Now I bet you're wondering what I do. No, I just don't sit around reading great romances all day, although I probably could. I own a little flower shop here. Actually, the only one, Peggy's Petals. How did I decide this was what I wanted to do with the rest of my life? Well. My husband, he was never great with words. Instead, he used to shower me with the most beautiful arrangements for my birthdays, anniversaries, and for all those silly I'm sorry moments. He said he spoke the language of love with flowers. So, I decided after he passed to open this small flower shop. It genuinely makes my heart happy to see those happy as they pick up arrangements or are surprised with one. So, now, I help those to speak the words that are scarce, through the language of flowers.

I will not lie. I'm hesitant to even send this letter, and perhaps I won't. Perhaps I'll write it, show it to Trinity, and then shove it in the garbage. In which case, you won't be reading it. To be honest, Trinity is secretly hoping my pen pal will be a man and that he'll sweep me off my feet as the heroes do in the books I read. I've told her that those things don't happen to people in real life. She just shakes her head and smiles and tells me they must because authors must get their inspiration from somewhere. In her defense, she just reunited with her long-lost love, so she is still living that high.

Anyway, I don't know if you are a male or female, if you too, like me, are widowed, divorced, or are living content with the love of your life. All I can say is that I am writing this letter hoping to find a new companion, a friend. I'm hoping for one that I can share things with, and I'm telling the truth when I say that I'd like to get Trinity off my back. *Laughs*

If you are interested in writing back, I welcome you to do so. If not, I hope this letter finds you well, and that it serves as a friendly voice if you are in search of one.

I will watch for a letter in the coming weeks, but again, there is no pressure.

Peggy Hollis

I put the letter down and took a moment. Then I went back to the start and re-read the letter again. Something about this was so real, so raw that I was curious to know more about this Peggy. I reached into my side drawer and pulled out the small notebook I kept there and a pen and began writing my response to her.

Peggy

Glancing out my front window, I could see some of my neighbours were already up and about on this beautiful spring day. It was Tuesday. Normally, I'd meet Trinity for coffee at The Crispy Biscuit, but she'd already told me that this week wouldn't work. She was busy at the store getting ready for her upcoming inventory blowout sale. Since Vi had moved into the retirement home and Trinity had taken over, she'd been finding boxes of books in storage. Books that Vi had ordered and forgotten about, or ones that simply had been packed up because they hadn't sold.

I grabbed my coat from the hook behind the door and slipped it over my shoulders. I'd decided I would head over to The Crispy Biscuit and grab coffee and a sweet and take them over to Trinity's instead. Knowing her, she probably hadn't even had breakfast this morning.

I'd just rounded the corner and spotted Thomas, Trinity's boyfriend, loading up his truck with wood. He'd started up Jenkins Woodworks right after selling his parents' ranch and hadn't looked back. In fact, Trinity said he'd been so busy he couldn't take on any more orders until some of the ones he had were off his plate.

"Morning, Peggy," he greeted me as I approached his truck.

"Morning, Thomas. How are things?"

"Can't complain. Finally got the rest of my wood order in. I was getting worried that I wouldn't be able to deliver those shelves you asked for until the end of summer."

I'd ordered some new custom-built shelves for the flower shop, something that would hold vases and other items that I wanted to display. "No worries. Whenever you get to them. I'm in no rush."

"Nope, you'll have them on time, as promised. If I had needed to travel down to Cedar Landing to get the wood, I would have." He smiled.

"No need to do that. I know you have a lot on the go. I can wait. After all, you gave me a tremendous discount."

"Well, thanks for being understanding. However, Trinity said you had to have them on time." We both laughed. "She told me get them done or I work morning, noon, and night until they're finished."

"Did she threaten to take away your breakfast again?"

"That and a few other things I won't mention." Thomas smiled as my cheeks heated.

"Oh dear." I laughed. "Was she home when you left? I thought I'd go down to The Crispy Biscuit and take her a coffee and something sweet."

Thomas nodded. "Yep, she was working away on organizing the boxes I found in my workshop. Vi had a ton of books that she never sold. Every time I find or open a box, I pray it isn't more books. We hope they go in this sale."

"It would be nice. I know she had found a bunch after Vi moved into the home. It might be nice for her to donate them to the home if they don't sell."

"Now that, Peggy, is an idea."

"Well, I'll suggest it to her when I get there."

"Please do. Did you want a ride? I'm almost finished up here. Shouldn't be but a few more minutes, then I just have a couple more stops to make after this."

"No, it's beautiful today. I'll walk."

Thomas nodded just as Joe Higgs came out with another cart full of wood. "All right, Peggy, see you later."

"Mrs. Hollis." Joe nodded.

I smiled and continued on my way. The Crispy Biscuit was packed by the time I got there. It was normally busy on Tuesdays, but today seemed busier. After winning the Festive Treasures Bake-Off, a day didn't go by that Brooke and Tristan didn't sell out of their pastries. Her baking boxes had taken off as well.

"Morning." I waved as I stepped inside to find an exhausted-looking Brooke standing behind the counter talking to Tristan.

"Hey, Peggy," they both greeted.

"Looks like business is booming." I smiled.

"Sure is. It's not even summer yet and we can barely keep up with the demand. I don't know what it will be like when tourists begin passing through," she said, giving me a small smile. "I may need to reconfigure the kitchen and hire bakers. "What can I get for you?"

"I'd like two large coffees, and I think I'll take the last two blueberry lemon scones. I know Trinity and I have been waiting for those."

"You and others in Willow Valley. It seems they are a favourite that I'd add to the year-round menu if I could get blueberries at a decent price," Brooke said as she typed the order into her computer first and then turned to grab the scones while Tristan poured the coffees. They'd turned into an amazing team after the Bake-Off last year. Rumour was there may be a wedding announcement coming soon, but they had announced nothing yet.

"It makes them extra special that they aren't available year-round." I smiled.

"That's what I told her," Tristan said, placing the

coffee down on the counter and putting the cups into a tray. "Is Trinity not coming in this morning?"

"No, I'm headed there now. She is working on that huge inventory blowout she's having. I guess Vi had been storing books like a squirrel stores nuts. She's been finding books everywhere." The three of us laughed.

"Oh well, tell her to bring some flyers down and we will put them up on the community board," Brooke said, nodding to the bulletin board that was packed with advertisements.

"Will do. Thanks, guys. I'll see you later." I waved, picking up the small tray and bag and heading to the door.

I was about to push the door open when I spotted Alexa Flores approaching. She smiled as she pulled the door open for me. "Good morning, Peggy." She smiled.

"Morning, Alexa. How are things with the new business?" I questioned. Alexa had moved to Willow Valley just after Christmas. She was working in the interior design business and had partnered up with Serenity Johnson, the real estate agent.

"Oh, busy as ever. I just picked up a couple more clients. It's been slow, but it's picking up now that word of mouth is spreading. Serenity has been helping a lot."

"That's wonderful. So glad to hear it."

"Thank you."

"Well, if you need flowers for anything, you know where to find me."

"I will. See you soon," she said, waiting for me to step outside before she headed into The Crispy Biscuit.

It only took me another ten minutes, but I was finally standing outside of Bluebird Books. I could see Trinity at the counter sorting through boxes, a frustrated look on her face. "Never fear," I called as I stepped inside, "your coffee and treats are here." I smiled, holding up the small bag.

"Peggy." She smiled, coming around the counter to take the coffee from my hand. "This is a wonderful surprise."

"Figured maybe you could use a bit of a break. Why don't we sit down?"

"You have no idea," she said, looking exhausted as we both made our way over to the two large wingback chairs that sat in the front of her store and took a seat. I removed one scone from the bag and passed it over to Trinity, while she pulled the coffee cups from the holder and passed me mine.

She sat back, took a bite, and closed her eyes while she chewed. "Oh...this is good." She mumbled, "I haven't eaten since breakfast, and you couldn't have picked a better option."

"Yeah, I figured this would be the best choice. I ran into Thomas on my way as well. He said you were working hard, getting ready for this sale."

"Oh, Peggy, there are sooo many books," Trinity cried.

"So, so, so many. I honestly don't know what Vi was thinking when she just stored them away. If I'd have known she'd stuffed them up in the loft where Thomas now has his workshop, I'd of sold them off a long while ago. So much money in inventory, just sitting there."

"I was thinking, if they all don't sell, what if you were to donate them to the home afterward?"

"I never thought that far ahead, but I think that is a marvelous idea."

"I'm so glad. I thought of it as I was talking with Thomas this morning. I remembered you told me that the home could use books to help fill their library. The last time I was out there dropping flowers off, I noticed how empty the shelves were."

"Well, we will see what I have left. It's a fantastic idea." She took another bite of her scone. "Oh, and I got a response to my letter I sent. I've received a lovely young girl by the name of Valerie to write to."

"Oh, wonderful." I smiled.

The room grew quiet as Trinity studied me. "Did you get one?" she questioned.

I shook my head, focusing on my scone. "Nope, guess maybe they don't want to write to a stranger either." I shrugged.

Without responding, she let out a sigh, got up from her chair, and made her way around the counter. "Peggy?"

"Yes?" I said, turning to see her standing there with a bit of a worried look on her face.

"Don't be mad, okay?"

I frowned. "Why would I be mad?" I shrugged, not knowing what Peggy was talking about. Then I noticed a sealed envelope in her hand. Embarrassment, worry, and then fear ran through me. "What is that?"

Trinity chewed her bottom lip for a minute, almost as if she were considering not telling me what was in the envelope. She came around and sat down in her chair, leaning forward to gather my full attention as she passed me the envelope.

"What is this?" I questioned, looking down at the envelope with my name on it.

"I noticed the night we went to drop off our letters that you were acting strange. I didn't notice until after you left for the washroom that you had dropped your letter into the garbage pail instead of into the box. I wasn't snooping. I just went to throw something in the garbage and caught the logo on the envelope. Anyway, I put the letter you wrote into the box. I figured, well hoped, that perhaps it fell, and you didn't see it." She smiled. "The look on your face tells me that you slipped it in the garbage instead. I had a hunch you would do that." She winked.

I looked down at the envelope in my hand and looked back at Trinity. The letter hadn't fallen; I had deposited it in the garbage. I wasn't ready to do this, and since she knew me so well, she'd caught me.

"That is a response to your letter. Melinda asked me to deliver it to you, since she hadn't seen you in a few days," Trinity said, holding out the letter for me to take. "Are you mad?"

I let out a breath. "I suppose you've read this?"

Trinity shook her head. "No. I wouldn't do that. I'd never read your mail, but I think you should have it. Honestly, I just think this will be a good thing for you."

I nodded, looking down at my name written on the front of the envelope.

"Are you angry?" Trinity asked again.

I shook my head. "No, I'm not mad. This is just weird. It was such a struggle to come up with what to say in the first letter. I can't imagine telling them any more, especially when I don't know them."

"Well, the good news is it's just a letter. Read it, respond, and know that you're never going to meet. Make things up or you can bear your entire soul to them and never worry about things biting you in the butt. Honestly, he or she is literally a safe stranger. Forever."

Rain was coming down as I finished up the last of the dinner dishes and placed them back in the cupboard. I had gotten home this afternoon and dove right into this week's order sheets. I needed to make sure that I had everything in stock before I began making the arrangements that were ordered.

I'd just sat down at the table to order things I needed when the letter Trinity had handed me caught my eye. It sat there, still sealed, waiting for me to open it.

When she'd brought it over to me, I'd cringed. Someone had read my letter, a stranger. I'd allowed Trinity to, but there was nothing in there that she didn't already know. But a stranger... The thought of it was the reason I'd thrown the letter away. After all, who wanted to know about little Peggy Hollis?

I blew out a breath and picked up the envelope, flipping it over and over in my hand, before pulling at the small, lifted corner and tearing it open. I pulled out the letter and opened it, staring down at the handwriting. I didn't even need to read a word on to know it was a man.

I threw the letter down, my stomach in knots, and went over to the counter. Lifting the already boiled kettle from its base, I poured the hot water over the tea bag that sat in my mug. Then I grabbed the mug and the letter and made my way over to the couch. I flipped the small light on and sat down.

Grabbing the blanket off the back of the couch, I

threw it over my legs and opened the letter again, getting comfortable to read it.

Dearest Peggy,

Thank you for the wonderful letter and for sharing some things about yourself. My name is Ethan Alexander. I'm a 29-year veteran in the Marines. A Seargent Major and will be soon celebrating my retirement. It's been a wonderful career, one that I'd do again if given the chance. People would say I'm crazy, but the opportunities this position has provided for me are one of a kind.

Like you, I don't know many people. Well, aside from the men and women who serve under me. I have buried myself in my career, and now that I'm facing retirement, I know that meeting people will have to be something I get used to.

Also, like you, I lost my wife. She'd taken ill, and although she fought with all her might, she could not win her battle. After that, I too turned inward. It's a hard thing to deal with, losing someone, but don't be like me. I shoved many people away, including my daughter, because looking at her was like looking at her mother. We are currently working on repairing our relationship and I am grateful each day for her.

Do you have children?

What sort of things do you like to do in your spare time? I don't have a lot of spare time in my current rank; I get two days off per month, and I basically use them for sleeping. Like you, I read. I'm a huge true crime fan and love the occasional political thriller. Is romance all you read?

The flower shop... I'm interested. You say you help people speak the language of love through flowers. I'm curious... can you give me an example? I remember my wife always telling me that her favorite flower was honeysuckle... care to shed some light on a guy who is flower illiterate?

I look forward to your next letter; I am going to count on you as my first connection outside of the Marines. Let's learn together how to be friends with one another. No pressure on one another. If the mood strikes, we write a letter. If two months pass before one of us responds, that is okay too. Seriously, no pressure. I think perhaps we both need this.

*I hope to hear from you, but if I don't, trust
me, I understand. I'll be watching for the mail.
If letters take too long, you can always email
me. I'll include my card in the envelope with
that address for you.*

Ethan

I folded the letter and placed it on the table, debating
what to do. Should I write back, should I not? I grabbed
the envelope and found the small card inside with his
email address on it. I flipped the card over in my hand and
then grabbed the letter and went back over to my
computer where I quickly put his email into my contacts.
Then I went back to placing my flower order.

Weeks had passed, the store got busy, and soon I'd
forgotten all about the letter. One afternoon, I was
working on an order. I noticed the person who'd ordered
had requested the arrangement contain honeysuckle. It
was then I'd remembered the letter. I grabbed a handful
from the cooler and smiled to myself as I finished the
arrangement. I'd sat down at my small desk and picked up
the little card and quickly wrote exactly what the client
had asked, then set the arrangement aside for Carl to
deliver.

When I sat back down at my desk and pulled out a few
bills I was getting ready to pay, I found the letter from
Ethan was the second item in the pile. I'd remembered

bringing it with me one day to write back, and it had gotten lost in the mess of things on my desk. I stopped and read the letter again. Instead of paying the bills, I grabbed my notebook and pen and began writing my next letter, only five weeks later.

Ethan

July 2023

"Mail call!" Sanders yelled. I placed my mug down on my small desk. I grabbed the pile of letters from Peggy and shoved them into my duffel bag. I hobbled over to where Sanders was handing out the mail and waited, hoping that Peggy had written to me in time. We'd taken to emailing, but every once in a while, she'd still send a letter via the mail, and if my count was correct, the next letter should arrive by snail mail.

I'd injured my back shortly after I'd sent my first letter. I'd sought medical attention right away, but it didn't seem to heal as quickly as they first thought. In fact, the military doctor had talked to me about retiring early. Giving up wasn't something I'd ever done, and I fought through the last two months, but I knew the writing was on the wall.

"Here you go," Sanders said, handing me a lone letter. I flipped it over and recognized the writing immediately.

"Thanks, Sanders."

"Make sure you take it easy, Sergeant."

I nodded and made my way back to my desk. I looked around my room; I was headed home tomorrow, wherever that may be, six months sooner than I'd planned. I'd fly back into the US, to Texas, where I'd begin the discharge process and get everything set up for my retirement. From there, I'd set my plans in motion.

I ripped open the envelope and pulled the letter out. Unfolding it, I began reading.

Dearest Ethan,

Sorry for the delay in responding. Things have picked up around here. I had to hire another delivery driver, and I brought on another student, so I have two now instead of one. It's been so busy I haven't even had time to read. Did you get the books I sent? Like you, Thomas enjoys reading political thrillers, and when he suggested them, I knew they were ones you'd need to read.

Oh, and all that talk and worry over my estimate for the summer festival... well, you are looking at the person who won the bid! That's right, I won the bid to do all the garden arrangements and planters for the summer festival. Talk about excited. I've already begun the planting in the gardens, and I've been planning out the planters. It's been very exciting to work on such an amazing project for the town.

Thank you for giving me the courage and push to apply. It was your nothing ventured comment that forced me to push the send button, just so you know. Even Trinity bribing me with skittle cookies didn't do it. Which you need to try one day. They are to die for. Another Tristan creation!

Oh, and I've included a picture so you can see what I've done so far. It may not look like much, but it's taken weeks and many, many hours of planning.

I pulled the picture from behind the letter and looked at tall the gardens. Pink, purple, and white flowers in assorted arrangements in all the gardens popped in front of the dark-green bushes. I smiled. I was proud of her for hitting that submit button. From the pictures she had sent me in the past of her work, I knew without a doubt she'd pull this off without fail. Putting the picture down on the desk, I returned to the letter.

I'm sorry to hear about your accident. I hope your back is healing and that you'll be back to your regular duties. I know you were worried about them discharging you and forcing you into early retirement, especially with you being so close to retirement. I'll send some prayers upstairs that doesn't happen.

As for the continuation of learning the language of flowers, we will now look at the pink rose. Pink roses are genuinely associated with femininity. Its meaning is grace and sweetness. Some others associate them with gentleness, appreciation, joy, thankfulness, and elegance. They are honestly perfect for pretty much any event and are one of my best sellers. Next letter we will talk about the green rose.

Anyway, I look forward to hearing from you, I'm curious about how you're healing. Until our next letter....

With love,
Peggy.

I folded the letter and placed it back in the envelope, along with the picture. Then I opened the top of my duffel bag and put the letter with the others, and the emails I'd printed.

I'd been back in Texas for almost two weeks, and I stared down at the plane ticket on my table. I got up from the chair in my small apartment on base and gathered up the ticket, shoving it into my document holder when the phone rang.

"Hey, Dad," I heard as I picked up the phone to be greeted by my daughter's voice.

"Hey, Melinda. How's everything?"

"Going well. So, have you decided where you're headed yet?"

"Not sure just yet. I still have a few more things to get in order before I decide. I also have paperwork to sign with the Marine Corp, which I am doing this afternoon," I said, flipping the ticket over in my hand, debating telling her now what I'd already decided.

"Oh. Well, let me know once you decide." I could hear the disappointment in her voice.

"Will do. I'm going to be late for a meeting. Can I call you later tonight?" I questioned.

"Yeah, Dad. I'll be home from work about eight."

"Talk to you after that, then."

"Sure thing. Love you, Dad."

"Love you too, kid."

We hung up, and I glanced at the pile of letters from Peggy that lay on the table. I removed the last letter and sat down, sending a response via email. She didn't know that I'd returned to American soil. I'd planned on heading to Cabo in the coming weeks to enjoy some sunshine and spend a few months unwinding. However, something inside me told me Willow Valley was where I needed to be. Like my daughter, she also didn't know that I'd confirmed my decision to head to Willow Valley.

After all of our letters, all of our discussions, it was only a few letters ago we'd begun talking about perhaps meeting one day. I chuckled as we both agreed that we'd be nervous. It was when she finally told me she was looking forward to that day, should it ever come, that I knew I had to do it. That was the day I'd bought my ticket.

I stared at the wooden sign that read Willow Valley Bed and Breakfast from the back of the cab. I couldn't believe that I was here, sitting in the driveway of this small-town bed-and-breakfast.

"Sir, that will be thirty-five seventeen," the driver said from the front seat.

I reached into my jacket pocket and pulled my wallet out, shoving some cash at the driver, and then climbed out of the backseat to meet him as he pulled my bags from the trunk. I looked down at my small pile of personal objects and picked up the two bags, heading to the front door of the inn.

I pushed open the front door, the smell of lilac hitting my nose. An older woman stood behind a small counter, folding some towels. She looked up at me and smiled. "Welcome to Willow Valley Bed and Breakfast. What can I do for you?"

"Thank you. You should be expecting me. Ethan Alexander," I said, placing my bags on the floor at my feet.

"Oh, yes." She nodded, pulling a book in front of her. She ran her finger down a list of names, finally stopping on mine. "Your room is located right at the top of the stairs, dear. Room number seven. You should find it quite comfortable. If there is anything you need, just ask," the elderly lady said as she searched a drawer for the key.

"What time is dinner?"

"Oh, we serve dinner at five every night in the dining

room. I used to do separate meals, but since I hurt my hip and my dear Harry took ill, I just don't have the energy any longer."

I glanced down at my watch. It was shortly after six. "Any chance there are any leftovers?"

"Oh, my dear, sadly, you are our only reservation tonight. We had more, but they got pushed to arrive later. I have some cookies, though," she said, making her way down the hall to what I was sure was the kitchen and returned with two cookies wrapped in cellophane. "If this isn't enough, The Crispy Biscuit is only a short walk away."

"Perfect," I muttered, not wanting to be rude as I looked at the two small cookies that would never fill me.

I made my way up the stairs to the room I'd been assigned. I slid my key into the lock and opened the door. The room was basic, with a king-size bed, small TV, a small writing desk, and a small bathroom. There was a large wingback chair beside the window, and I placed my bag beside it and looked out the window. The inn sat up on a hill, and from the window I could look out over the small town. I stood there for a moment, and then my stomach let out a large growl.

I unwrapped the cookies and shoved one in my mouth, followed by the other. There was no way the two small cookies were going to cure this hunger, so instead of unpacking, I grabbed my jacket, locked the door, and made my way to The Crispy Biscuit.

I'd just finished the last mouthful of beef stew when Cici, the young server, approached my table to refill my coffee.

"How was that stew?" she questioned. "Was I right?"

"Perfect. Just what I needed after a long day," I said, glancing over her shoulder to see if Melinda had come in.

"Can I interest you in some desert? I've noticed you can't stop checking out the pastry counter."

It was true, I had been looking over that way, but not because of the pastries. I smiled. "Oh, I was hoping Melinda would be here."

Cici looked at me funny. "Oh, are you a friend of hers?" she questioned, frowning, a little hint of protection in her voice.

"I'm her father. I decided I wanted to surprise her. She doesn't know I'm in town. I'm Ethan," I said, holding out my hand.

"Oh, why didn't you say so? Melinda is off tonight. She was doing some work on her program."

I smiled. "I see. Well, please, don't let on that I'm here. It's a surprise."

"No worries, your secret is safe with me." She winked. "So, what sort of desert would you like? We have some wonderful cinnamon buns, or perhaps a piece of coffee cake?"

"I'll take a slice of coffee cake, please." Cici was about to walk away when I cleared my throat. "You wouldn't be able to give me directions on how to get to the nearest flower shop, would you?"

"Sure can," she said, leaving me and bringing over a piece of coffee cake with the directions scribbled on a piece of paper. "If you're heading over there tonight, I'd get going soon. I believe Peggy's Petals closes at eight."

I glanced at my watch. It was a little past seven. I slid my fork through the cake and took a bite and requested my bill.

Peggy

"Is this the correct way to have done this?" Sarah asked as she held up the mixed rose arrangement she'd been working on. "It doesn't look like yours."

I walked over and checked it. "Well, you can add a bit more foliage to it. But overall, I think it looks gorgeous."

"Oh, I got the arrangement for Mr. Ryan done as well," Trisha said, coming out of the cooler.

"Oh wonderful. I'll check that over before Tristan picks that up. Oh, and remember, girls, tomorrow, we head out to the park and get to work on the last garden bed," I said, beginning to clean up after what seemed to be a long day.

"What time did you want us here?"

"I'd like to get an early start. Say six. That way, we can

get that bed planted before the sun hits the field. It won't be so hot then. Plus, I can get back here to open for ten."

"Sounds good. Did you want help to clean up and with closing tonight?"

"No, you girls put things in the cooler you were working with and then head out. I'll take care of everything else."

I left the girls and headed out to the front of the store, quickly clearing the flowers that were out. Then I grabbed the small green wagon that sat in the corner and headed out the front door. In the summer, I always placed buckets of fresh-cut flowers outside to help draw in customers. I began placing the buckets into the wagon and pulled them inside and took them to the back. I pulled the cooler door open and began putting them in their places, making sure everything was neat for the morning.

I'd just shut the door to the cooler and said good-bye to the girls when I heard the door chimes go off. I glanced at my watch; it was quarter to eight. Normally, I never had a customer past seven, unless it was an emergency. I wiped my hands on my apron and headed out front. At first, I didn't see anyone, until I looked farther around the corner. There, a broad-shouldered man with very short, neatly cut dark hair stood inside the store, studying the flowers in the cooler. I couldn't stop my eyes from roaming from his broad shoulders to his fit waist to his perfectly framed ass in the pair of jeans he wore. He wasn't from around here, that much I knew.

"Can I help you?" I asked.

The man turned and smiled at me. "Yes, I'd like to order some flowers."

"Oh well, I can certainly help with that," I said, taking a step closer to him, his cologne invading my senses. It was then I noticed his fully tatted, muscular forearms.

"I'm also looking for Peggy," he said, his ocean-blue eyes meeting mine. "Do you know if she is still here today?"

A funny feeling came over me as I looked into his eyes. Looking at him, it felt as if I should know him. "I'm Peggy," I said, swallowing hard. "And you are?"

"Peggy! It's wonderful to finally meet you. It's me. Ethan."

I was tired, and I searched my brain, trying to figure out who it was I knew by that name. I stood there studying him and then it hit. "Ethan?" I asked, my eyes widening as my stomach flipped.

"Yes, Peggy, it's me," he said, opening his arms.

Completely shocked that the man I only knew through letters stood in my shop, I stepped into his open arms and hugged him. When I felt his arms release me, I stepped back, my cheeks on fire as we looked at one another. He was so handsome, almost too handsome for me.

"What are you doing here?" I questioned. "I mean, I thought you weren't due to return for at least another six months?"

"Well, sadly, my back didn't heal as fast as I'd hoped, and the doctors advised me to take an early retirement. You mustn't have gotten my last email."

"I haven't checked, but I'm sorry to hear that. How are you feeling now?"

"A little sore, but I took part in some rehabilitation programs when I returned, and they helped a lot."

"That's great," I said, staring back at him, still shocked he was standing in front of me.

Again, the silence grew stronger as I stood across from Ethan. His eyes against his dark hair and complexion stood out. It was almost hard to look away. They were mesmerizing. He'd mentioned that in one of his letters, but I figured he was exaggerating. He was not. I felt as if I were frozen to the spot, and then I remembered he'd wanted flowers. I cleared my throat. "So, the flowers?"

"Yes. They are for someone special," he said, watching me intently.

"Okay, um. Let's see." I stepped toward the cooler door and pulled the bucket of multi-coloured pink roses along with some greenery and baby's breath. I focused on what I was doing so that my hands wouldn't shake. I carried the bucket to the counter and began building a bouquet."

"Ah, pink roses. Seems fitting, as that was where we left off in the lessons of roses," he said.

"Oh, did you want another colour? What would be better?" I questioned, leaving the roses to go for a different one.

"No, no, they are perfect," he said, smiling.

I nodded and continued putting together the flowers. Once finished, I looked at Ethan and held up the full vase. "How is this?"

"Gorgeous," he whispered, his eyes meeting mine.

I swallowed hard, trying to calm my nerves. "Now for the card." I reached for one of the small notecards and a pen. "What would you like it to say?"

Ethan stood there for a moment, still watching me, and then he cleared his throat. "Melinda, to new beginnings."

I'd begun writing the instant he started talking, and I paused when I got to the end of the little note and the words registered. Melinda? There was only one Melinda in Willow Valley, and she had to be twenty years younger than he was, if not more. I looked up at him, a look of confusion on my face.

"Love, Dad," Ethan finished, grinning at me.

"You're...you're Melinda's father?" I questioned, shocked at the information I'd just found out. Melinda had rarely spoken of her father, until the pen pal program began. Until then, all we knew was that she'd lost her mother, and that her father was in the military, but that was all.

"I am. Who did you think I was, her boyfriend?" Ethan laughed.

His laugh was just as I'd imagined. "Oh goodness, I don't know what I was thinking," I said, feeling my cheeks heat as I smiled and met his eyes. The room grew quiet once again.

"You know, you're really pretty when you smile. I mean, you're beautiful anyway, but when you smile, wow, you light up the room," he said, his eyes dancing.

I didn't know how to respond. Instead, nerves fluttered through me. I reached for some hot-pink ribbon and cut a piece from the spool. With shaking hands, I began tying it around the neck of the vase, then placed the card in a holder and shoved it inside.

"Well, welcome to Willow Valley," I said, knowing full well my cheeks were the same hue as those roses. I could barely look at him. I wasn't used to compliments, at least not from such a handsome man.

"Well, Peggy, I won't keep you. I know that it's closing time. What do I owe you for the flowers?"

I waved my hand in front of my face and shook my head. "Those are on the house. It's the least I can do for you."

Ethan stood there still watching me as he reached behind him and pulled his wallet out from his pocket. He flipped it open and pulled money out and dropped forty dollars onto the counter. "Well then, this is a tip for a very generous flower shop owner. Who I very much look forward to getting to know better in the coming days. If she is interested, that is?"

I stood there shocked at his words, as his eyes fell to the floor and climbed up my body before grabbing the vase. When he left the store, I walked over to the front window and watched as he walked down the street. I swallowed hard, not believing that Ethan Alexander had really been standing in my store. "I'd love to get to know you, too," I whispered, a little too late for him to hear, and with shaking hands, I reached for the lock on the door.

I practically ran down the street on my way over to see Trinity. Out of breath, I banged on the front window of Bluebird Books. Startled, Trinity looked up, a look of relief coming over her face when she saw me. I'd called her earlier in a panic after Ethan had left, begging to come and see her. I was rambling so much she probably had no clue what I was even talking about. She stepped out from behind the counter, rushed over and unlocked the door, letting me inside. Luna slept soundly on the top of the chair, her usual spot, and I patted her head as I walked past her.

"All right, do you want to tell me what the panic was all about?" Trinity questioned, emptying the last of the coffee from the pot into two cups. "You called me up and acted as if the shop had just been robbed. I've been on pins and needles waiting for you to get here. In fact, had you not of shown up in a few minutes, I was going to send Thomas over to make sure you were okay," she said, worry filling her eyes.

I ran my fingers through my hair and looked at my best friend.

"Well, are going to say something?" Trinity asked again. "You look like you've seen a ghost."

"Get a pen pal you said," I said breathlessly.

Trinity laughed. "I said that, yes. Now what else?"

"You'll never meet him, you also said."

"What, is Ethan coming here, to Willow Valley? How wonderful. The four of us will have to get together and go to dinner."

I dropped my head to the counter, still not believing that only a half hour ago he'd stood before me in my flower shop, looking good enough to eat. I didn't know what was worse, the fact that he was really here, or the fact that when I laid eyes on him, I noticed something happening in my body.

"Are you going to keep me in suspense forever?" Trinity questioned, taking a sip of coffee.

"He's here. In Willow Valley. In fact, only half an hour ago he came into the store and ordered flowers."

"Oh. That's interesting," Trinity said, grinning at me, her chin resting on her hand. "And..."

"And...and he is Melinda's father."

"Ah, so he came to visit his daughter. That is sweet."

I shook my head. "He also came here to see me. He told me he looks forward to getting to know me over the course of the next few weeks."

"Peggy, that is fantastic, and very exciting. What are you guys going to do? Oh, you could take him to the summer festival. Oh, and you could join Thomas and I for dinner too during the festival."

I let out a sigh. "Despite what you might think, this is not fantastic!" I cried.

"What do you mean?" Trinity looked at me, shock lining her face.

"Trinity, it's horrifying. He came into my shop and caught me at my worst. I mean, look at me, I'm a mess. I've been working all day. My hands are a disaster, all the dirt under my nails...my hair is a mess, and well, my clothes, they aren't exactly flattering." I grabbed the legs of my oversized jeans and pulled on them as I looked down and noticed a stain on my T-shirt that I must have gotten from lunch.

Trinity giggled. "Oh, look at this."

"Look at what?" I asked, panicked.

"I'm shocked that you actually care?"

I looked over at my friend, who sat there with a cheeky smile on her face. She was enjoying my torture, I knew it.

"Of course, I care. If you had of seen him, you'd of cared too."

"Good looking?" she asked, sitting down on the stool behind the counter.

"You've got no idea," I said, thinking back to those muscular and fully tatted arms, and those eyes, those shoulders.

"Earth to Peggy," Trinity said, waving her hand in front of my face.

I frowned. "He totally snuck up on me like some sort of stalker."

Trinity let out a loud laugh. "I hardly think he is acting like a stalker. In your letters, you told him what you did. I know because I read it. So, you volunteered that information in the very first letter. So, it's not stalking. It reminds me of that Christmas book we read at the book club a couple of years ago. Oh goodness, what was the title?" Trinity questioned, drumming her fingers on the counter.

"You mean Coffee Shop Love at Christmas?" I questioned.

"Yes! Did you know they made that into a movie? It was on last Christmas, actually."

"I did. I watched it."

"Now I think you need to go home and either watch it or reread it. You are going to need guidance from your characters on this," Trinity said with a straight face, even though I knew she was laughing on the inside. "Actually, I have a copy I can give you." She looked around at the stacks of books behind the counter.

I rolled my eyes. "Goodness, this isn't like that movie."

"Sure it is. This is going to turn out just like one of your novels. I can feel it!"

I rolled my eyes, not believing what I was hearing. Was she dismissing my dilemma and telling me to take advice from a movie or book plot? I took a sip of my coffee just as the back door opened and Thomas stepped inside.

"Hey, Peggy. Trin, what are we doing for dinner?"

"Oh, there is a shepherd's pie upstairs in the oven. Guess who's in town?" Trinity asked Thomas.

Thomas looked from me to Trinity and shrugged. "No clue."

"Ethan Alexander." Trinity grinned, looking over at me.

Thomas frowned. "Who the hell is Ethan Alexander?"

"Just the man who is going to steal this woman's heart," Trinity said, looking over at me, smiling.

I'd known Trinity had been dying to play matchmaker. From the letters Ethan and I had shared, I knew it was completely possible, too. Our discussions over the months in those letters had brought us together in a way that I probably wouldn't have found possible if we had met in person. Even though a part of me was scared, and if I could ever look him in the eyes, I knew I was looking forward to getting to know Ethan Alexander. When I returned home that evening, I sat down at my computer and replied to the email he'd sent me a few weeks ago.

Ethan

I glanced at my watch, fixed the collar on my shirt, and looked myself over one more time before grabbing the vase of pink roses. I'd called Melinda last night after returning to find out what she was working over the next few days. I'd hoped I'd done so without giving it away that I was in Willow Valley.

Approaching the front window of The Crispy Biscuit, I stopped and looked inside. Immediately, I saw her standing beside a table taking an order. She smiled at both women before walking away. That smile took my breath away, just like her mother's did the first time I'd seen it.

I took a breath and made my way into the diner, taking a seat against the wall. I placed the vase on the table and picked up the menu, somewhat hiding behind it.

"Ah, it's you," I heard a voice say.

I turned to see Cici standing there, smiling at me. "Morning, Cici."

"Morning, sir. I take it you are here to see Melinda?" she asked in a hushed tone.

I nodded.

"And you're here to surprise her. Give me a minute." She winked. "Oh, and I'll bring over the coffee."

Minutes later, I looked up into the face of my daughter. I could tell from her expression that she was shocked.

"Dad, what on earth are you doing here?" she questioned, her voice full of excitement, eyes full of tears.

"Hey, sweetie. Good to see you," I said, standing up and hugging my daughter for the first time in fifteen years.

"You too, Dad," she whispered as she hugged me so tight, I didn't think she'd let me go.

"These are for you." I pointed to the flowers on the table and watched her eyes light up once again.

"They're beautiful," she whispered, sitting down across from me.

Just then, Cici appeared with two cups and the pot of coffee. She filled both cups and then looked at Melinda. "Take your time with your dad. I got this," she said, looking around the quiet diner.

Melinda smiled. "Thanks, Cici, I owe you." Then she turned back to me. "I'm shocked you're actually sitting here. I'm so happy to see you. It's been so long."

"That it has. Too long, but now it's time to make up for that." I winked.

Melinda grew quiet as she looked at me. "So, for real, what brings you to Willow Valley? You aren't sick, are you?" Panic lined her eyes.

"No, I'm not sick."

"Last time we spoke, you were planning to go down south and live it up somewhere. You sure you're all right?"

I chuckled. "Melinda, I'm not sick. I really wanted to reconnect with you. It's been too long, and it sort of hit me over the past few months. I'm retired now. It's time to find out who my daughter is. Get to know her again and settle my ass down. So, as nice as a vacation in Cabo would have been, I had a change of plans."

"Well, Dad, as wonderful as that is, and I am glad you are here, please try again." she said, winking at me as she leaned in and smelled the roses.

"Wow, can't put anything past you, can I?" I chuckled. Melinda was just like her mother. Not only was she beautiful and confident, but she, too, could see right through my shit.

"Dad, as much as I would like to think that I am the only reason you came to Willow Valley, I have to be honest with myself."

"Okay, just know that I came here to see you, but also, my pen pal lives here."

Melinda looked at me. I could see her already

searching through her mind, trying to figure out all those who took part in the program so she could narrow down who it might be. I said nothing more. I just allowed her to sort through the mental lists she'd already made.

"Oh my," she whispered. "Okay, there was Trinity, Brooke, Ava, Amanda, Mindi....goodness...so many," she said, counting the people on her fingers. Then she looked over at me. "Most everyone in town that took part is married or in a relationship, Dad." She went back over the list one more time. "I give up. Are you going to tell me who or are you going to leave me sitting here in suspense?"

"Peggy," I replied, waiting to see her reaction.

"Peggy? As in Peggy Hollis?"

"Yes, and I already went to meet her. That's where the flowers came from," I said, nodding to them.

"I see. How did that go?" she questioned, giving me an odd look, as if she knew something I didn't.

I shrugged. "Well, I know I shocked her. I mean, in our letters we talked about perhaps meeting one day. Then I show up out of the blue."

"I'm sure you shocked her." The look on her face confirmed what I was thinking.

I nodded. "Maybe it wasn't the wisest move."

"Probably not. She's a widow, Dad. I know we all have been on her to date, and I know Trinity had begged her to join in the program to find a guy to date. I feel partially responsible for this, because Peggy didn't put her letter in the box to send. Trinity did. Peggy had thrown it in the garbage, and to be honest, I knew that and so I never should have put her letter in that bag."

I frowned, wondering why she would have done that. "What? Why would she put it in the garbage?"

"Oh, Dad, I don't know. She is a wonderful person, really she is. Just don't get your hopes up that things will work out with her, or that something will come of this."

I looked at my daughter. "Well, at least I can spend time with you. I mean, if you'll let me."

Melinda smiled. "Of course, I will. I'm thrilled you are here. Now, saying that, as much as I shouldn't meddle, I'll also help you with Peggy. I mean, she wrote back to you, and obviously has been writing to you since. So, if you have screwed up to start, perhaps I can help you fix it."

"I'd appreciate that. Your old man needs all the help he can get, to be honest."

Cici came over, and Melinda ordered us both a plate of bacon, eggs, and hash browns. "Breakfast should be out soon."

"Perfect. So tell me, where are you living?"

"I have a wonderful little apartment a few streets over."

"And this is The Crispy Biscuit?" I said, looking around. "You like it here, right? I mean, they treat you well??"

"You know they do. I love working here. Brooke, my

boss, has given me a lot of additional responsibilities now, and I am working hard at gaining more. I just love it here. Such a breath of fresh air."

I nodded. "Are you seeing anyone?"

Melinda shook her head. "No, Dad. I am career focused, and with all the extra work on that program, I don't have the time. Honestly, between here and there, I have very little time to date anyone."

Melinda continued talking about work and life here in Willow Valley while I listened intently. I was almost finished my breakfast when she stopped speaking and looked up at me, a smirk on her face.

"What?" I questioned.

"I can't believe you. Showing up at poor Peggy's house like a stalker. Dad, that is creepy."

"In all fairness, I truly wasn't stalking her."

"What would you call it then?" she asked.

"Well, let me see. We exchanged many letters, we got to know one another, and I knew her address. We'd talked about perhaps meeting one day. I guess you could call it..." I tapped my fingers on the table, trying to come up with a word that would make sense. However, I didn't have time as Melinda sat across from me, shaking her head.

"Well, Dad, we women would call it a stalker." She giggled.

I smiled at my daughter. I knew she knew I had no intent of harming anyone, especially Peggy. "Well, call it whatever you want. If you want to call me a stalker, so be it, but I will tell you I hope I haven't ruined a chance at getting to know her."

Melinda looked at me thoughtfully. "You like her that much?"

"Yes, I do. I enjoyed reading every one of her letters, to where I began looking forward to them. I felt as if I were getting to know her. To be honest, when I saw her, it was as if I had known her forever."

"Okay, so I guess you really want some help then?"

I nodded my head and stabbed at the remaining hash browns on my plate.

"Okay, so this is how we will do this. You will start by taking her breakfast this morning," Melinda said, smiling at me.

"I wouldn't have the first idea of what she even likes. How am I going to take her breakfast?"

Melinda laughed. "Dad, you forget, your daughter works in the most popular locations in all of Willow Valley! We also serve breakfast, in case you didn't realize that." She pointed to my plate. "And you are in luck, because I've served Peggy more breakfast than probably anyone in this town. Also, she called twenty minutes ago and ordered breakfast for delivery. I was going to run it over myself, but I'll have them fix up her order and you can take it to her," Melinda said, laughing.

"You're sure about this?"

Melinda nodded her head, her body language displaying a world of confidence. "Trust me. Then after you take her breakfast, don't go see her again."

"What?" I asked, confused. "Why wouldn't I go see her again?"

"Oh, Dad...really? Because you are just going to continue sending her letters. You're going to win her over with words. You two still write, don't you?"

"Yeah, but it seems silly to send a letter when we are in the same town."

"Do you have her email?" she questioned.

I nodded. "Yes, we emailed sometimes too, especially if I was in a place without mail access."

"Perfect!" She grinned and leaned forward. "Okay...so hear is the plan...."

I smiled as I sat there while my daughter devised me a plan to get to know Peggy better.

Peggy

I stood behind the counter working on an order for Alexa, or Alex as she preferred to be called. She'd left a message last night saying she would be in this morning to pick up an arrangement of carnations for an open house that Serenity was running. I was just about finished when she stepped into the store.

"Morning, Peggy," she greeted.

"Morning, Alexa. I mean Alex. I am just about finished. Just have a couple more things to add to your arrangement. Serenity called and changed a couple things last minute."

"No problem. I'm early anyway. Serenity also asked me to pick up one of these bears for a baby's room that I've staged."

"I just got some new ones in. Take a peek."

She walked over and looked at the pile of bears I kept in the corner. I normally used them for Get Well arrangements or for children. She pulled one bear from the shelf and set it on the counter.

"Perfect," I said, smiling as I picked up the arrangement and placed the vase into a clear bag before I brought it over to the counter.

"Peggy, that is beautiful. I think Serenity is going to love it."

I smiled as I looked at the arrangement. "I hope so." It was a mixture of dark-red and variegated light-red carnations, greenery, and baby's breath. The choices had been the perfect selection for this order, as she stated she wanted something simple. "I think she is going to love the bear you chose."

"Thanks. She really wants to get this house sold. She said it's been on the market too long for her liking, but then she says that all the time." Alex rolled her eyes and then giggled. "I'm hoping it will help me also. The more people who see what I'm capable of with staging and interior design, the faster I'll build."

"My dear, you are going to do just fine."

"You sound exactly like Serenity." Alex smiled. "Although we have a few exciting listings coming up."

"Yes, I saw Serenity the other night as I was leaving the grocery store. She mentioned the same thing. Don't forget to bring over any flyers you want added to the community board."

"Great! I'll let her know." She grabbed the bag and the bear and walked out the door, waving as she went.

I made my way over and pushed the door open, placing the little wedge underneath so I could get some fresh air inside. I grabbed the small wagon I'd pulled from the cooler and began setting up the displays outside. I'd just finished and glanced down the road to the left and then the right and immediately spotted Ethan heading this way.

My stomach fluttered with nerves as I watched his tall, powerful frame walking toward me. He'd been in town for over two weeks now, and aside from the morning Melinda had him bring me breakfast, the only contact I'd had with him was through email, which I thought was weird for someone who said they wanted to get to know me better.

I adjusted a couple of pails of flowers and then made my way inside, determined to make myself look busy. Then I remembered Melinda lived right around the corner from me, so perhaps he was going to visit her. Either way, I needed to be prepared, I thought to myself.

I made my way into the small bathroom and glanced at my reflection in the mirror. I ran my hands over my hair, making sure that there were no fly-away strands. Then I looked at my nails. Just as I suspected: dirt. We'd spent the morning out at the park, planting the rest of the flower planters for the summer festival. Despite wearing gloves, the dirt had done a number on my hands. I grabbed the small nail brush from under the counter and quickly began scrubbing away as I caught my reflection in the mirror.

"You are being so silly. He's probably going to see Melinda," I whispered to myself, continuing to scrub away. When I finished, I stepped out of the small bathroom and made my way over to my work area. I quickly checked my email, once again seeing nothing from Ethan. I let out a breath and turned my focus to the next order when I looked up and met the eyes of Ethan Alexander.

He looked even better today than he had the first night he'd stepped in here. He wore a pair of well-worn jeans and a black shirt that brought out his blue eyes. The scent of his cologne was taking over the store, enveloping me at the same time.

"Good morning, Peggy." He smiled, stepping closer to the counter where he placed a bag from The Crispy Biscuit. "I went to see Melinda this morning. Thought I'd bring you breakfast..." He shoved the bag toward me.

I reached for it and opened the paper bag. I could already smell the cheese omelette and bacon. "Thank you, but you didn't need to do that."

"I know I didn't. I wanted to."

"Thank you. I had an early start this morning and

didn't have time to have anything." I smiled. "We finished the last of the planters for the festival."

"Well then, eat up." He winked. "Can't have a busy day without being fully prepared for it."

Shyly, I removed the container from the bag and opened it. Taking the fork, I dug into the hot cheesy omelette. While I took another bite, Ethan walked over to the cooler and began looking inside again.

"How did Melinda like the flowers?" I questioned. "You never did tell me."

"She loved them. I do, however, need another arrangement."

"Oh? For Melinda again?"

"No, not for Melinda this time. I'd love it if I could get a yellow rose bouquet, but I don't see any here. Do you not have them in?"

I put my fork down and nodded. "Oh, that is because they are in the back of the cooler. Just came in yesterday. I haven't had time to bring them out yet. How many stems?"

"Twelve please."

I went around into the back of the cooler and grabbed twelve yellow roses and a little greenery and came back around to the counter, where I quickly assembled them. "Did you want them in a vase?"

"Yes, please."

I tied a cute yellow ribbon around the vase and placed it up on the counter. "What about a card?"

"Yes, please."

"Would you like me to fill it out like I did last time? Or would you like to do it?"

"You already know your writing is better than mine, so I'll have you do it." He chuckled. "I'm surprised you could even read my letters."

"Well, I won't lie, it took me some time, but I got used to it." I winked, meeting his eyes. I wasn't sure I would ever tire of looking at them. They were so clear, and today they reminded me of sea glass. "Okay, for the note, what would you like it to say?"

I pulled out the chair at the small desk and picked up my pen, waiting for him to begin.

"Um...let me think." He paced back and forth. "Dinner. Tonight. 7:30. Pick the place. It's on me."

I stopped writing and looked over my shoulder to see him grinning.

"What do you say? Will you have dinner with me?"

Immediately, I felt my heart melt. This had to be the sweetest, most romantic thing anyone had ever done for me, and inside I felt my heart skip a beat. Was he for real? Was he kidding? He had to be joking, and while I waited for him to give me the punch line, I looked at him, not sure what to say.

Ethan cleared his throat. "What do you say? Do you have a favourite restaurant in town?"

I nodded. "I do. The Italian Affair, just a couple blocks over."

"Does 7:30 work for you?" he asked, leaning on the counter as he waited for my response.

I nodded.

"Okay, I'll pick you up at 7."

His eyes glued to mine, he took a couple of steps backward and then turned, still looking over his shoulder at me. When he was gone, I turned and looked down at the small card I'd been writing, reading what I'd written once again as a warm feeling came over me. He wasn't kidding, he really did want to take me for dinner.

I worked around the shop for the next couple of hours. Each minute that passed, the excitement grew. Then the nerves crept in. I had just finished dealing with a customer when I spotted the card that I'd been writing out to go with the yellow roses. As I stared at the words, the nervousness grew. I hadn't been on a date in so long, I wasn't sure I even remembered what one was like. Immediately, I ran to the phone and dialed Trinity.

"Hello, Bluebird Books!" she sang over the phone.

"I don't know what I've done," I blurted without a hello.

Trinity giggled. "What are you talking about?"

"Ethan! Ethan Alexander, remember, the pen pal I'd never meet? The safe haven, as you called him."

I heard a mumble in the background, followed by another, and then the line went quiet. "All right, spill it. What is going on now?" she asked with laughter in her voice.

"Well, Ethan was here. He asked me out on a date!"

"OOOHHH tell me more…"

I could imagine Trinity rubbing her hands together like she was gearing up, once again, to begin a project she'd been dying to work on. Which she was, and that project was me. She'd been so disappointed when I told her that he hadn't been around and had only been emailing, I thought she was going to cry. I was certain she was probably grinning like an idiot and bursting with excitement at this development.

I swallowed hard. "I did something dumb. I said yes. I, Peggy Hollis, agreed to go out with him. What was I thinking? First, he shows up here like some stalker, then disappears and reverts to email for two weeks, and this morning he brings me breakfast and asks me out on a date."

"He brought you breakfast?" Trinity questioned. "Again?"

I let out a sigh. "Yes."

"Did you order it again for delivery?"

"No, and he brought me my second favorite, that super cheesy omelette."

Trinity was quiet for a moment, and then I heard her whisper, "You know, Peggy, I have a good feeling about this."

Trinity was happy with this development, excited that the plan I knew she had created in her mind was clearly working.

"I don't. This can only end in one way."

"Oh stop."

"What! I'm being serious."

"You are ridiculous. Now, where are you going?"

"I don't know. I'll probably end up in a body bag somewhere in a dumpster."

Trinity let out a laugh. "Oh gosh, no you won't. Now tell me, where are you going for dinner?"

"To the Italian Affair."

"Oh, they are so good. What time, and honestly, how do you even know it's a date? I mean, perhaps he is just looking for friendship."

"Yes, they are great. They have great food. I know it's a date because he is paying."

"Free food from the Italian Affair and you are complaining. What is wrong with you?" Trinity giggled.

"What's wrong with me?" I thought for a moment. "I don't date!"

"Well, you do tonight." She giggled.

Mentally, I sifted through my closet, wondering what the hell I should wear. I hadn't bought a new dress in years. The only new clothes I'd bought in the last few years were baggy jeans and T-shirts. I'd even decided to stop buying sexy undergarments and had talked myself into granny underwear.

"So, what are you going to wear?"

I put my hand on my forehead. "That's just it. I have no idea. I mean, I haven't bought a new dress in years. I just mentally sifted through my closet and there is nothing. Perhaps I should call him and cancel."

"Peggy, you will not break a date—an important date," Trinity said in a stern voice. "I'd be so disappointed."

I went quiet on the phone, not sure what to do. "Okay, fine, I guess I'll go shopping," I said, giving up.

"We will find you something. I can meet you downtown in twenty minutes. Ava just got here."

"Make it thirty. The girls should be here by then," I said, finding it odd that Ava had just gotten to the store when she normally didn't work today. I wouldn't have put it past Trinity that, while we were talking, she sent a text to Ava, saying it was an emergency and asking her to come in.

"Okay, see you then."

"Wait!" I yelled, trying to get her attention before she hung up.

"What on earth is it now?"

"Is this even safe?" I questioned. I was panicking, I knew it, but part of me couldn't stop.

"Is what safe? Shopping? Of course! What is the matter with you?"

"No, not shopping. This date? Tonight? Ethan Alexander?"

Trinity laughed into the phone. "Goodness, Peggy. It's worse than I thought."

I frowned. "What is?"

"You! You need this date more than I thought. The man is a marine, for goodness' sake. He is perfectly safe."

"No, you are wrong. He *was* a marine. He's retired now," I said, feeling satisfied that I'd proved her wrong.

"You are being ridiculous. Of course, he's safe." Trinity laughed. "Get a grip, would you?"

"Ha! I have a grip! A very strong grip on reality. The Golden Gate Killer was a police officer, and I've heard that Ted Bundy was a very personable guy. Just because he was a marine doesn't make him safe."

The line went quiet, and if I listened hard enough, I

was sure I could hear Trinity roll her eyes. I also knew she was probably silently laughing at my panic.

"Okay, Thomas and I will head to The Italian Affair for dinner tonight and spy on your date to make sure you are fine. That way, you'll have witnesses."

I let out a laugh. I knew she was joking, but I also knew she would do that in a heartbeat if she thought it would get me on this date.

"Fine, I will be fine!"

"Yes, you will! Now, go get ready. I will meet you outside of Peach Street Boutique in a half hour, and we shall find you something sexy for tonight."

I stepped out of the changing room, feeling uncomfortable, and looked over at Trinity. She'd made me try this dress on, and she didn't give up on it the entire time we'd been at the shop. It was the only one I didn't want to put on, and as soon as I'd stepped out of the small room and she looked at me, a smile came to her lips.

"My friend. My beautiful, stunningly gorgeous friend, that is the dress!" She squealed with excitement. "This is the dress!" she repeated, this time running her hands over the fabric.

I looked down at myself and then at the mirror. The green dress hugged me in every place I wasn't used to showing off anymore and hadn't been since before Darren had passed away. "I don't know," I said, fidgeting as I looked at myself in the mirror.

Trinity's reflection appeared in the mirror behind me, and she smiled at me as she ran her hands over my hips. "Ethan will love this on you. Who knew you had these curves hidden in those oversized jeans and T-shirts you wear?" She giggled, running her hands over my hips again.

I could see the sincerity in her eyes as she studied my reflection. "Fine, you win again," I said, laughing as I threw my hands up in the air. "I'll get this dress."

"YAY!!!!" Trinity laughed as she hugged me tightly. "I'm so excited for you."

"I'm glad someone is excited. I'm going to take this off now, get back into my comfy clothes."

"You aren't any fun, Peggy Hollis," Trinity called, still smiling at me.

"I can't believe, in a few hours, you're going to be sitting down to dinner with Ethan, and you better not leave anything out. You hear me. I want every nitty-gritty little detail," Trinity said as we stepped out of the boutique and headed down the street toward Bluebird Books.

Shifting the bag to my other hand, I turned and

looked at my best friend. "I swear, if this turns out bad, you and I are going to have to have a chat."

Trinity pulled me in for a hug. "Well, hate to break it to you. We won't be able to."

"Why not?" I questioned, looking at her with confusion.

Her eyes full of laughter, she looked at me. "Well, according to you, you'll be in a dumpster somewhere." Trinity laughed.

I looked at my friend as tears ran down her face. Then I too started laughing at how ridiculous my own words sounded.

Ethan

I was on a high as I left Peggy's shop. Melinda's plan had worked. It was two weeks of wanting to see her, but we emailed instead, and then I did as my daughter suggested and asked her out. Peggy had said yes, and I felt like less of a stalker than I had when I'd spoken to my daughter earlier. As I walked down the road, I decided that I'd take a walk through the small town. I wanted to familiarize myself with the area, something I hadn't done yet.

Eventually, I'd found The Italian Affair. I entered the small restaurant and made a reservation for tonight. Then I continued my walk. I passed many places that Peggy had shared with me in her letters. It was nice to see them in person, see the actual building now in my mind. Some she'd described them to me so perfectly that they looked exactly as I imagined.

After a long walk, I made it back to the Willow Valley Bed and Breakfast and was greeted by Bessy, the owner.

"Ah, Mr. Alexander. Will you be joining us tonight for dinner? We're having roast chicken, roasted potatoes, fresh asparagus from the garden out back, along with a recipe from my very own mother. Her Amish buns. People always tell me they are to die for. Brooke has been on me to give her the recipe for The Crispy Biscuit, but I refuse."

"Well, that sounds amazing. I sadly will not be here to join you for dinner. I have a date." I smiled.

"Oh." A light blush lined her cheeks. "A date, you say?"

"Yes."

"I remember when Harry and I used to date. It's been years, of course, and now with his failing health, well..."

I smiled at Bessy. She must be in her early eighties, I figured, and wondered how she kept up with the running of this place.

"Where are you headed with your date?" she questioned. "Anywhere I'd know?"

"Just over to The Italian Affair."

Bessy's eyes lit up. "Well, you picked a wonderful place. Best Italian food in the entire area. I hope you enjoy."

I smiled. "And I hope Harry takes you on a date soon!" I winked.

"Oh goodness, our days of dating have expired. When

you get to be our age, well, you're just happy you can continue doing what you're doing every day."

I smiled and nodded, asked her a few more questions about some places here in Willow Valley, and then made my way upstairs to my room. I walked over to my closet and opened the door. I hadn't a clue what I would wear tonight. In the military, we would just use our dress uniform. I somewhat missed having that. I never had to think about what to wear.

I pulled out a pair of black dress pants and placed them on the bed, then I sifted through the shirts that hung color-coded in the closet. Pulling out two shirts, I held them both up. Perhaps this would be too dressy, I countered. This one, from the look of the place, would be too casual. I let out my breath and pulled out another two shirts, faced, once again, with the same problem.

"Yep, I miss my uniform," I muttered, throwing the shirts into a heap on the bed.

Walking over to the small desk in my room, I picked up the phone and dialed Melinda's number. I was just about to hang up after the fifth ring when I heard her answer.

"Hello!"

"Melinda! Can you do a favour for your old man?"

Melinda laughed. "Of course, Dad. What do you need?"

"Can you come over here and help me find something

to wear for tonight?" I asked, closing my eyes at the thought of involving my daughter on my date.

The phone went silent. "Tonight? What's tonight?" she questioned.

"Well, I did as you suggested, and I have a date."

"She said yes?" She squealed with excitement. "Dad, that is wonderful. I'm so happy for you."

I chuckled. "She did. So what do you say? Can you help your old man out?"

Within the hour, Melinda arrived, and I now stood beside my daughter as she sifted through my shirts, looking for the perfect one. She'd hold each one up to me and shake her head, then pull the next one out and repeat the process.

"What did you wear before?" She sighed, going back to a shirt she'd thrown down in a pile on my bed as a maybe. "These are so old. The patterns, even the fabric is different than the ones in the stores here."

"Well, whenever we had a function or a dinner out, we wore our dress uniform. It was simple. I never had to guess what to wear. I'd just pull that out. It was simple. The way I like it. To be honest, I didn't have many dates though, kid."

"I see." She shook her head, completely focused on the task at hand. "I think this one might do," she said, holding up one of the few shirts I hated.

"No, not that one. I should have told you that from the start when you threw it into that pile."

"What is wrong with this?" she questioned, looking down at the other options she'd set aside. "It's probably the most practical."

"For starters, it's got a lot of white in it. We are having Italian."

"Are you telling me that the sergeant is a messy eater?" she asked, pulling out another shirt.

"When I'm nervous and not on my game, yes," I answered.

"You know, Dad, for what it's worth, I am sure Peggy is just as nervous as you are."

"What makes you say that?"

Melinda shrugged. "Well, I don't think the woman has been on a date since she lost her late husband. She's probably feeling sick to her stomach with nerves."

"Do you think so?"

"I do. How did she act when you brought her breakfast this morning?"

"She was surprised. Didn't get angry like I thought she would."

"And the flower order?"

"I'm not sure. I think she really liked it, but it was hard to tell."

Melinda looked at me with a smile on her face. "It got you

the date, though, so I'm guessing it must have gone well. Give yourself a little credit. Otherwise, we wouldn't be standing here trying to find you something to wear. Try this one on."

I took the hanger from her and stepped into the small washroom, quickly changing into the dress pants and shirt. I glanced at myself in the mirror and then opened the door.

Melinda took one look at me. "That is perfect!"

"It is?" I said, looking down at myself, still wishing I had my uniform.

"Yes, your eyes pop in this. Women are a sucker for eyes," she said once again with confidence. "Also, roll up your sleeves. You have muscular arms, and the tattoos just add to them."

I couldn't believe I was standing here having my daughter tell me what women liked. "You know, I'm not dead. I do know what women like." I chuckled.

"Okay then, why have you not done it yet?" she said, looking at me with laughter in her eyes.

While I rolled my sleeves, I watched as she hung all my shirts back up and then turned to me and nodded. "Not bad, if I say so myself," she said, bringing her hand to her cheek. I could see she was contemplating something, and that scared me.

"What is it?" I questioned.

"I hate to break it to you, Dad, but I also think we need to go shopping soon. Get you some new clothes."

She stepped forward and removed a piece of lint from my perfectly pressed shirt. "I can even ask Cici to join us if you like."

I shook my head. "No to Cici joining us. I can only deal with you." I chucked. "Now can I ask another favor from you?" I questioned.

"Of course."

"Do you think I could borrow your car for tonight? I was planning on walking, but I hear that it's supposed to rain."

"Well, I don't see it being a problem. I mean, gas it up and make sure you have it back to me by eleven, latest, midnight," she said, her voice stern, as if she were the parent and I were the child.

I glanced over at my daughter, unsure if she was joking or not, and then she broke out into laughter. "Sorry, Dad, I couldn't help it. Of course, you can. I was just joking around."

"Thanks, kid," I said, pulling her in for a hug. "Thanks for everything."

I stood in front of the full-length mirror in my bedroom and shook my head as my gaze landed on the curves of my hips. How had I let Trinity talk me into this dress? I gently pulled at the fabric that clung to my body. I'd closed the shop a little early, come home, showered and now stood here, almost cringing at the choice I'd agreed to.

Why on earth did I agree to this? I let out a sigh and made my way into my small kitchen and looked around. The place was clean, but it was old and in desperate need of repairs and a fresh coat of paint. I opened the scratched-up cupboard door and pulled out a glass, quickly filling it up with some juice from the fridge.

Perhaps one day I could find a better place to live, I thought to myself. This place was cramped. I'd bought practically the first house I'd seen and had moved from a much larger home into this.

I'd taken another mouthful of juice when the phone rang. "Hello."

I silently hoped it was Ethan. Perhaps he too had decided that this was a bad idea and was calling to cancel.

"Oh, I am so glad you haven't left yet," Trinity said into the phone.

"Why?" I questioned, alarm filling me. "Did you hear something about Ethan? I was right, wasn't I?"

"You're doing it again," she said, irritation lining her voice. "Everything is going to be fine."

"I know."

"I called because I wanted to say good luck." She giggled. "I hope you have a wonderful time."

I looked out the front window in time to see a car pull into my driveway. I frowned. It looked like Melinda's car. "Well, you called just in time. I believe he might be here."

"Okay, I will let you go. Have fun. Don't do anything I wouldn't do."

I laughed. "You mean, anything you wouldn't do now?"

"What does that mean?"

"Well, if I recall correctly, you too had your share of apprehension when Thomas returned."

"That's because I thought I knew what he was all

about." She giggled. "Turned out I was very wrong, but that's not a subject we need to talk about now."

I heard a firm knock on the door. "Okay, I've got to go," I whispered and hung up before Trinity said anything else.

I smoothed my dress down over my hips, removing any wrinkles that may have appeared, and walked to the door. Grabbing the door handle, I noticed my hand shaking, and I stopped to take a breath and calm myself down. When I opened the door, Ethan stood there. His eyes ran down the length of my body and back up before meeting my eyes.

"Hi, Peggy." He hesitated for a moment, his eyes once again looking me over.

My stomach dropped. This was the wrong dress. I knew it. My stomach flipped with nerves, and I felt self-conscious. I shifted from one foot to the other, wanting to run and change before we left.

Ethan cleared his throat. "You look stunning."

I felt my cheeks heat as we stood there, and somewhere inside of me, I felt a little more comfortable in this dress. Ethan looked handsome, dressed all in black. It brought out his piercing blue eyes, which I loved looking at. I also noticed his strong tatted forearms. It was as if he'd stepped off the pages of one of my books. A surge of excitement ran through me when I noticed his eyes roam over my body once again.

"You ready to go?" he questioned.

I nodded. "Just let me grab my purse."

"Sure thing."

As I pulled the door shut and locked it, a loose piece of window trim fell onto the porch. Immediately, I went to grab it, but Ethan beat me to it. "Looks like this needs to be repaired."

"Oh, yes, it's been broken for a while. I'll get around to fixing it, eventually," I said nervously, taking the wood from him and putting it back up over the window from where it had fallen. "Isn't this Melinda's car?" I questioned, trying to take the attention off my rundown old place.

"It is. I asked her if I could borrow it. I had to sell mine before I left for overseas. There really wasn't much point in having a car here when it was just going to sit and rust."

"That's true," I replied. "That would just be a waste."

"Yep, when I left, Melinda wasn't old enough to drive yet. So, I couldn't give her the car."

"How old was she when you left?" I questioned.

"Thirteen. I had to work to support her. So, after Polly passed away, I sold our place and our vehicles. I left shortly after that, and Melinda went to live with her aunt and uncle."

"Wow, you really just let go of everything?"

"I did. I had to. It was the only way I knew how to

move on. The only thing I regret about that decision is that I wasn't here to see my daughter grow up. I missed out. But there is time to rebuild what we lost."

"Did you find you moved on okay after that?"

"I did. Healing somehow seemed easier. Didn't you find that after you moved here?"

"In some ways, yes. In other's not so much." I shrugged.

"How so?"

"Well, I gave up the life I knew for a life I didn't. It was a big change, leaving a lot of our friends behind."

"I could see that. I guess I was lucky because I already had two lives that I knew. I was just giving one up that I'd never see again, but I was going to spend time with my other family, which in some ways felt more like home than life with my wife. I know what you're going to say, that it doesn't sound like things were good between us, but they were."

"Oh, I'd never say that. I'm not one to judge. Relationships, no matter how good they are, all have their difficulties."

"That they do and thank you for not being judgmental. Oh, and I made reservations for eight. That was the earliest I could get us in," I said as we walked down the front steps and by my car.

"Is this the car I've heard so much about?" he questioned as we stood there looking at my rusted-out vehicle.

"It is. It needs some repair work, too," I said. "It also just started making a funny noise a week ago."

"What does it sound like?"

"Oh, I can't explain it." I shrugged. "I was never good at that."

"Well, I'd be happy to take a listen if you'd like."

"Thanks." I softly smiled at him. "I appreciate that, but to be honest, I'm a little scared at what it might be."

"That's understandable. Car repairs can be costly." He nodded as he led me to his car. "What year is it?" he asked, opening the door for me to climb in.

"It's almost nine years old," I said as I pulled the belt across me.

Ethan nodded, closed my door, and walked his way around the car and climbed in. "Well, Peggy, there comes a time when you need to decide if the repair is worth it. Perhaps it's time to get a new car. I mean, you mentioned in one of your letters that it needed some repairs a few months ago. I recall you telling me those too cost a hefty price."

"I know. I'm thinking about it. I'm just a creature of habit."

Ethan backed out of my driveway and headed toward the main street. I glanced at my watch, noticing we'd only been together for ten minutes. It was a long while until we hit our reservation time. I cleared my throat. "So, what did you want to do before we head to the restaurant?"

"Well, I thought perhaps you could take me and introduce me to your friend, Trinity. I'd love to check out her bookstore. I'm in need of a new read."

Oh, how I wished he didn't ask me that, yet I still guided him over to Bluebird Books, where he parked in front of the store.

He came around to my side of the car and helped me out, then placed his hand on my lower back as he guided me to the store. I pulled the door open, and we both stepped inside, only to hear Trinity call from the back, "Be out in a minute."

"The thriller section is right here," I said, nodding to the wall of books just inside the door.

"Look at that. It is right next to the romance section. Might be kismet." He winked, pulling me against him.

I smiled and was about to say something when I heard a box fall to the floor and turned to see Trinity standing there, her hair a mess, her clothes covered in a layer of dust, looking frazzled.

"What on earth?" I cried, rushing over to help her.

"Oh, don't mind me. I lost my grip on the box. I've been digging around again in that back room." She laughed as she wiped the layers of dust off her clothing, then took notice of Ethan. "Oh, you must be Ethan." Trinity stepped over the mess on the floor and came around the counter to shake his hand, while I bent down to pick up the books that had fallen out of the box.

"You must be Trinity. I've heard lots about you."

"All good I hope," she said, smiling as she glanced over at me. "Peggy, leave the mess. Don't get your dress dirty," Trinity said, rushing over and knocking the books from my hand.

"Of course. Peggy speaks highly of you."

"Ethan needs another thriller to read," I said, trying to get their conversation to stop immediately. "So, I thought I'd bring him here."

"You better bring him here," Trinity said, placing her hand on her hips, giving me a look. "I wouldn't be very happy with you if you took him somewhere else."

"Well, you can be happy with me, because I brought him here."

"Of course, you did. Now, Thomas, my boyfriend, just finished reading this one." She went over to a shelf and pulled off a title, handing it to Ethan. "He told me it was one of Daniel Blizzard's best books yet."

"Ah yes, I've read his stuff before. I'll take it," Ethan said, stepping up to the counter.

"So, I hear you are having dinner at The Italian Affair?"

"Yes. Looking forward to a wonderful meal," Ethan said.

Trinity reached under the counter for what I was sure would be a bag, but she caught us both off guard when she stood up and snapped a picture of the pair of us with her cell phone.

"What was that for?" I questioned, horrified.

"Oh, you know, need to have a picture of the two of you, in case something happens to you, Peggy."

I rolled my eyes, but truthfully, I was ready to kill my best friend. I could feel my cheeks heating, but then Ethan let out a throaty chuckle. "Oh, Peggy, you never told me Trinity had such a great sense of humor."

"Yeah, she must have just developed it," I said, giving my friend a death stare. I didn't want Ethan to know what I'd said to Trinity earlier today.

The three of us laughed as Trinity packaged up the book that Ethan purchased. "Have a great night!" she said as she handed him the bag.

"We will. I promise I'll bring her back in one piece," he said as we walked out the door.

I glanced back over my shoulder at my friend and met her eyes. She fanned herself and mouthed, "He's hot."

Of course, I rolled my eyes and made my way out the front door of her shop.

We'd eaten our dinner and were now enjoying the rest of the bottle of wine we'd ordered while we waited for dessert. Dinner had been amazing, and the conversation had flowed as easily as one of our letters.

"So, what do you think so far about Willow Valley?" I asked as I looked into his eyes.

"It's smaller than what I'm used to, but it's very warm and welcoming. It's exactly how I imagined from your letters, and what Melinda had told me, to be honest."

"Really."

He nodded. "I could see myself settling here. It's been wonderful to have my daughter back in my life. To be honest, this little town is growing on me."

I smiled. "It has a way of doing that, for sure. Melinda is a wonderful girl. I think you may have been the reason she started the pen pal program, to be honest."

"That would be my daughter. She's been worried about me for a while, knowing I was getting ready to retire."

I smiled. "It's nice to have someone worry about you. Honestly, Ethan, she is a wonderful girl. She works hard. Brooke is lucky to have her at The Crispy Biscuit. I'd have hired her in a heartbeat if she hadn't already been working for Brooke."

For the first time since we'd sat down, the conversation grew quiet. I sat there, sipping on my wine, until Ethan cleared his throat.

"What was he like?" Ethan asked.

"Who?" I questioned.

"Darren. You barely spoke of him in your letters after the first one. I've told you a lot about Polly. Why don't you tell me about him?"

I shifted in my seat, a little uncomfortable with the question. Some would think I was ashamed of Darren, or that he didn't treat me well, but it couldn't have been further from the truth. I cleared my throat. "Well, he was an amazing man. Outdoors oriented. He was a hard worker, rarely complained, and loved his fishing time."

"How long were you together? I don't think you told me."

"We were only together six years, unfortunately. What about you and Polly?"

Ethan frowned as he looked at me, knowing full well he'd already told me they'd been married for fifteen before she passed away. In fact, he'd told me so many things about Polly, I felt as if I knew her. I just, for whatever reason, didn't want to talk about Darren anymore.

"Peggy?"

"Hmm, yes."

"Are you having a hard time talking about Darren?"

I brought my glass to my lips and sipped some of the wine, avoiding Ethan's eyes. How was I supposed to answer that? Of course, I was. I'd now been without him longer than I'd been with him. I felt his hand on mine and

I looked up to see him staring at me with kindness in his eyes.

"I know how hard it is," he said, his voice low.

A tear escaped my eye, and I pulled my hand away to wipe my eyes before the tear ran down my cheek, causing my makeup to smear. "I'm sorry, this year is just harder than it ever has been. Tell me it gets easier."

Ethan nodded. "It does. Hell, I still have those moments as well. Don't think for a minute I don't. I'll get thinking about her, about what could have been, and then suddenly I'm pulled into that pit."

"I'd never think that. You don't seem to be that type of person."

"I'm human. I think I just hide it better now."

I nodded, again growing quiet.

"Can I tell you something I don't think I've ever mentioned to another soul, not even to some of my most trusted and closest army buddies?" Ethan asked.

"Of course."

"The reason I left for deployment and constantly re-enrolled was because I couldn't look at Melinda. It took me a long time to get over the fact that it was like staring my wife in the face every time I looked at her. She is literally the spitting image of Polly. It's taken me this long to come see my daughter, to be able to be around her. It sounds horrible, and it hurts my heart to admit that. I have so much time to make up for, I don't know if it will be possible to do it. So, I understand what type of hard-ship speaking of Darren can be. Just know that I am still a safe place to talk, okay, even if we are sitting face-to-face instead of hiding behind a piece of paper. And know that if you can't say something face-to-face, you can always write me an email."

His words, his expression, the gentleness in his tone and eyes instantly won me over. I didn't feel pressured, I didn't feel forced, and I knew he was being sincere. He'd trusted me with a secret that he'd never told another soul. That spoke volumes.

"Thank you for trusting me with that. I'm glad you're here, and I am glad that you are getting back on the road to building a relationship with your daughter."

His eyes met mine, and he smiled. "Now, tell me, where is one able to buy a car around here? I can't keep taking you out in my daughter's car. That's just ridicu-lous." We both laughed. Then his expression grew serious. "If you want to go out with an older man like me again, that is."

I couldn't help but smile. It wasn't a secret Ethan was older than me by about fifteen years, although I didn't feel that when I spoke with him. He seemed to be no older than me. "There's a car lot out in Cedar Landing we could go to one day."

"Perfect. So does that mean you'd like to go out with me again?"

"I say I'd be more than happy to go out with you again."

"Perfect. Shall we?" he questioned, standing up and waiting for me to join him.

Ethan drove me home and surprised me by walking me to my door. He stood behind me, waiting, while I unlocked the front door, and then I turned to him.

"So, Sunday? Car shopping?"

"Sunday works."

"Okay, I will pick you up in the morning. We will head into Cedar Landing and go to the used car lot there," I said, shoving my keys back into my purse.

"Perfect, I can't wait. Thank you for joining me tonight," Ethan said, his voice low.

"You are welcome. I had a wonderful time, and I'm looking forward to the next."

The words had just left my lips when Ethan leaned in, his cologne invading my senses, and placed a gentle kiss on my cheek. I felt my cheeks heat and knew as he pulled away, he would see that I was, in fact, blushing.

"Good night, Peggy. Sleep well," he said, his hand still cupping my cheek.

"Good night." I stood there, a little shocked at what had just happened, and watched as he walked down my driveway to his car. Moments later, he waved good-bye as he pulled out of the driveway.

I opened the door and shut it again as I stepped into

the living room. I leaned up against it, locking it, and just stood there, letting the coolness of the old wood take the heat from my body. I could still smell his cologne as if he were right here.

As I stood there, my eyes closed, I wondered what it would have been like to have his lips on mine, kissing me. Was he a gentle kisser, or was he a demanding kisser? I let out the breath I was holding and opened my eyes, erasing those thoughts from my head. Then I hit the switch that shut the outside light off and made my way to my bedroom, where I got changed and crawled into bed. For the first time in years, I fell asleep to thoughts of a man who was not my husband.

Ethan

I sat in the large dining room of the Willow Valley Bed and Breakfast, a plate of bacon and eggs in front of me as I looked out over the large pond behind the house. It was a peaceful morning. Most guests weren't up yet, allowing me to have my breakfast in peace, which I was grateful for. I'd had a lot on my mind this morning after last night's date.

I already knew I'd like her. I'd been able to tell just from her letters. Then, when I'd first laid my eyes on her, I'd realized she wasn't only smart and had a kind heart, but she was gorgeous as well. I'd wanted to kiss her so badly last night, but I also didn't want to chase her away, so I'd settled for a small kiss on the cheek.

"Isn't breakfast to your liking, Ethan?" I heard Bessy ask as she refilled my coffee.

"No, it's wonderful. Just enjoying the morning scenery," I replied as I watched two mallards land on the pond and swim around.

"It is, isn't it?" she said, watching as well. "Those birds come here every morning. Swim for a bit and then they fly off. In previous years, they've nested here. I'm guessing with the increase in people fishing and picnicking in the area, they have decided it's not safe for them anymore. Then in the fall we are always visited by some deer, although last fall I only saw them twice."

"That's too bad."

Just then, two more of the guests appeared in the doorway and began loading their plates with food. Bessy excused herself and made her way to the table they chose and filled their mugs with coffee. I dug into my eggs and continued looking out the window, going back to my thoughts of last night. It was close to seven by the time I'd finished breakfast. I had to get Melinda's car back to her.

Fully gassed up, I pulled into her driveway and parked her car where it had been parked when I took it last night and made my way up the stairs to her apartment door. I knocked and waited.

"Dad? What are you doing here so early?" she questioned as she looked out at me.

"Early? Ha. I've been up since four." I chuckled.

"Oh, I forgot. Up with the sunrise." She shrugged and smiled as she opened the door farther, inviting me inside.

"Come in. You know it wouldn't hurt you to sleep in." She laughed.

"I apparently don't do that very well." I stepped into her apartment and glanced around. She decorated just like her mother did. It was a comfortable environment, and it felt peaceful. Everything had its place, with no clutter, so the place was practically spotless.

"Thank you for allowing me to borrow your car. I filled the tank for you," I said, placing her key in her hand.

"Oh, Dad, I was only kidding, but thank you." She smiled. "Want to come in? I just put on a fresh pot of coffee."

"Sure." I slipped my shoes off and followed her over to the small kitchen table. "Nice place you have here," I said, glancing around.

"Thanks. Would you like the grand tour?"

"Sure."

Melinda smiled. "Well, this is the kitchen."

I chuckled. "You are such a smart-ass. Reminds me so much of your mother."

"Good thing I got her sense of humor."

I laughed again. "Sure is, kid." I could tell she was incredibly proud of her place.

"Okay, and this is my living room. I watch TV and read here. Over here is my little writing desk. Brooke has given me the task of coming up with a new recipe for the bakery counter. It's not going very well, as you can see."

She giggled, picking up a pile of papers that had been scribbled on and dropping them back to the desk.

"You can do it," I replied. "I'm also happy to be the guinea pig anytime."

"Be careful what you wish for. In here is my room, and over there is another bedroom. Right now, it's got a spare bed in there, but I am thinking of turning it into an office or something equally exciting, like a craft room."

"Hey. Wait a minute. You have a spare room, and your old man is staying in a bed-and-breakfast? What the hell, kid."

Melinda laughed, causing me to laugh. "Dad, I like my space. Don't even think about it. You would not want to live with me."

I couldn't help but chuckle again. "There, you finally have some of me in there. I hoped I'd find it." I laughed. "Don't worry, I love my space, too," I said, wrapping my arm around her shoulders and pulling her in for a half hug.

Melinda grew quiet and held her hands behind her back, swinging her hips. I could tell she had something on her mind.

"What is it?" I questioned.

"Dad, do you think you are going to look for a place here?" Melinda questioned, leading me back to the kitchen, where she pulled out two mugs from her cupboard.

I thought for a moment. She'd asked me many times prior to my arriving and now again. "Never know. I will not say no. I am, however, going to tell you I have another date with Peggy on Sunday. We will see how this one goes."

"Wow, another one already? Are you thinking this might be something serious?" Melinda asked, raising her eyebrows, a smile on her face. "Are you also trying to tell me you'll only stay if you and Peggy get together?"

"No, that isn't what I'm saying."

"All right then. Just wanted to make sure."

"Anyway, yes, we have another one already. I can certainly see that there may be potential for more. She is a wonderful lady. Anyway, we are spending the day together, heading down to Cedar Landing to a used car lot. I need to find myself something to drive."

"I told you it's not a problem to borrow my car."

"I know, and I appreciate that, but I'll need a car eventually."

Melinda thought for a moment. "True. Well then, if you have a date on Sunday, then perhaps we should go shopping before that."

"What for?"

"Clothes."

"Perhaps." The thought of shopping for clothes made me a little queasy.

"Perhaps?" Melinda asked. "You are kidding, right?

I've already gone through your entire closet. You need something. New things."

I let out a sigh as I took the cup that she'd placed in front of me and took a sip. "If I must."

"You must. I won't take no for an answer." She placed her mug on the table and looked up at the clock. "What are you doing today?"

"Today?"

"Yes, Dad, today. I'm off, so maybe we should just get it over with. Gives you less time to think about going. Less time to back out of going. Besides, even these T-shirts you have are a little tight." She pulled at the fabric of my T-shirt.

I looked down at myself. I saw nothing wrong with what I had on. I looked at Melinda. The look on her face was the same one her mother used to have when she had already decided what it was I was going to spend my day doing. I blew out a breath, knowing there was nothing I was going to say to change her mind. "All right, if you insist. But I'm finishing my coffee first."

"Deal," she said, clapping her hands together.

I stood in the center of a men's clothing store just on the outskirts of Willow Valley as Melinda sifted through a rack of shirts. Apparently, I wasn't any good at dressing myself, or so she said after the last few things I'd picked out. So, I'd agreed to her choosing the clothing, and I'd try it on. So far, to my surprise, everything that she'd picked had been a success.

"All right, these are the last of these. Go try them on as well," she said, handing me another large lot of shirts and pants.

I'd gotten halfway through the pile when I heard her clear her throat on the other side of the change room door. "Dad," she whispered.

"Yeah."

"Promise me you won't kill me?"

"Why is it I'm worried about what you're going to ask me?" I chuckled.

Melinda giggled. "Probably because you will. How are you for dating underwear?" she whispered through the door.

I frowned. I came from a generation where underwear was underwear. We didn't have morning, day, night, and dating kind. "Um, kid, I don't know what that even is," I answered.

"Ugh. Figures," she said, annoyance in her voice. "Get with the times. It's underwear you'd wear on a date."

I pulled the door open to show her the next shirt and

found her standing in front of me with three packages of underwear in her hand.

"See. Boxers or briefs," she said, shrugging her shoulders as she looked at each package. "I don't know which you prefer, but you really need to have a few good pairs of dating underwear," she said, shoving the three packs at me.

I took them and looked at each one. "No blue. Not brown. I think I'll just stick with these," I said, holding up the boxers and shoving the other two packs of briefs at her and shutting the door. Suddenly, something hit me on the head. Shocked, I looked down at the floor to see a package of black briefs lying on the floor, a loud giggle erupting from the other side of the door.

"I take it those are for me?"

"Yes, black all the way, Dad," I heard Melinda say as she continued to laugh.

Peggy

I pulled into the driveway of the inn and waved at Bessy. She was sitting out on the front porch. I cut the engine and climbed out of the car and made my way up the front stairs.

"Good morning, Peggy. What brings you out here on your day off?"

I smiled as I saw the baby sweater she was knitting. "Oh, I came to pick up a friend, Ethan Alexander. I promised him I'd take him to Cedar Landing today to look for a car. "I see you're busy working on a baby sweater."

She held it up for me to see. "Yep. Thought I'd make it for the giveaway basket that Booke is raffling off for the festival. She brought over some baked goods from the diner for me the other day, for my birthday. I've already finished the matching hat and booties," she said, shuffling around in her knitting basket and producing the two little matching items.

"Oh, Bessy, they are beautiful. Brooke is going to love this addition. Whoever wins this basket is going to enjoy those. I could take them to Brooke if it's easier than you taking them over there?"

"Yes, Brooke called. I planned on taking them out myself, but not sure if I can get away with Harry being so ill." She shrugged, placing the booties and hat back in the basket. "I'm surprised that's these hands can still take all this knitting," she said, holding up her old hands.

I smiled. "You are doing fine. Have you found anyone to help around here yet?" I questioned. I knew Harry's health was in fast decline and that Bessy was having a harder time getting around. I also knew they had a lot on their plate with this bed and breakfast.

She shook her head. "Unfortunately not. I hired a lovely young lady to come in and do all the cleaning, but as for the rest of it, not yet. I fear that I may have to close the place if anything happens to Harry. If only Johnny hadn't passed on so young" she said, looking up at me, sadness in her eyes.

I nodded. "Yes, well, I will keep my eyes and ears open for you." There'd been a rumor going around in town that they may have to close the inn if they didn't get help. All their years of hard work building it to what it was today, it would be a shame to see that happen.

"Thanks, Peggy. I'd appreciate it. Trinity let me put an ad up on her community bulletin board, as did Brooke."

"Well, I am sure something will come of that." I smiled. "If you have another one, I can always pop it up on mine as well."

"That would be wonderful. I can get one for you."

The loud bang of a door shutting caught my attention, and I turned to see Ethan standing behind me, a coat flung over his forearm. "Morning," he said, leaning in and kissing me on the cheek in greeting.

"Morning. You ready to go?"

"I am. Looking forward to it. Bessy, good morning."

"Morning, Ethan. Enjoy your day," she said, going back to her knitting. "I'll get that ad for you too."

"Perfect, Bessy. I'll pick it up from you when I bring over the baskets for the porch."

"Sounds good."

We drove through Cedar Landing and finally pulled into the last used car lot on the street. I was happy that Ethan said nothing to me about the much bigger one on the other side of the road as we drove past it. "Hopefully, you can find something here. They have an excellent selection of pretty much everything." I pulled into an empty spot where the car sputtered when I put it in park and then cut the engine.

"What about that other lot we passed?" Ethan asked. "They looked much bigger."

"Oh, no, remember, I used to live here. You don't want to deal with that guy."

Ethan looked at me, then smiled. "What's wrong with that guy?"

"Oh, he's a tad bit shady." I winked.

Ethan chuckled, and we both climbed out of the car and looked around.

"Where should we start?" I questioned. "Do you have a preference? What it is you're looking for?"

"Well, let's look over there first," he said, pointing toward some trucks and SUVs. If we find nothing here, we can always check out the other lot. Perhaps it's changed owners."

Chills ran up my spine, and I shook my head. "It hasn't. Seriously, this is the best lot in the area. We will find something here," I said, my tone firm as I grabbed my jacket from the back seat and slipped it on and followed behind Ethan.

"Is there something wrong with that other lot?" Ethan

questioned. "I'm not afraid of a shady character." He winked.

"Aside from what I told you, no. I talked to a friend of mine that still lives here, and she said this is the place to look. The other one is much bigger but, with less choice. Plus, this one has better prices," I said as I pointed out a white pickup, trying to distract him, but Ethan shook his head.

"No white, gets dirty too fast," he said as we looked through the windows of some of the larger trucks on the lot. "This one is nice." He stopped at a black Ford F-Series.

I put my hand up to the window and peeked inside. "Oh, very nice. You'd look good in this, I think."

"You think?" Ethan asked.

I nodded. "I do." I shyly smiled.

Ethan pulled the door open and began looking inside the truck. Satisfied, he glanced around and waved over to a sales associate to inquire about the truck. We listened to him go over all the features, along with the specs that were completely foreign to me. Once finished, the three of us piled into the truck and took it out for a test drive.

"Is the price firm?" he questioned.

The associate glanced at me and then looked over at Ethan. "I'm sure there is some wiggle room."

We continued driving around, finally pulling back into the lot and parking the vehicle. Ethan handed the associate back the keys and told him he'd think about it. We walked a bit more, looked at a few more vehicles, when Ethan turned to me.

"You know, Peggy, I've always wanted one of those trucks. I think I might just see what kind of deal I can negotiate."

"Go for it. I'll run across the street and grab up a coffee," I said.

"Sounds good."

I watched Ethan head inside, and I took off across the street to the small coffee shop. I returned twenty minutes later with two hot coffees. I could see Ethan inside talking with the sales guy, so I walked over to my car and leaned against the hood. I was about halfway done with my coffee when I saw the door open, and Ethan approached me.

"How's it going?" I asked.

"Good, he is just getting the paperwork ready." He grinned.

I nodded. "I'm glad."

"You know, I was thinking back to all the letters we exchanged."

"Oh?"

"I was thinking back to the other day as well. You mentioning that noise your car was making? That was the noise we heard all the way here, wasn't it?"

I nodded. "Yes."

"I thought so. You know, it doesn't sound very good. I'm wondering if it's not an engine problem."

"Oh?" I grew worried at the serious expression on his face. "That's something major, isn't it?"

"Could be. I'm not a mechanic. Honestly, Peggy, perhaps it's time to make a change yourself. Put the money that you'd put into a repair toward something newer and perhaps under warranty."

I looked at my rusted-out car and shook my head. Panic filled me. Ethan didn't know what he was talking about. Like he said, he wasn't a mechanic. "No, this car is very reliable."

Ethan nodded. "I'm sure it is. However, while we are here, I could help you choose one. I can probably get you a great bargain too. I mean, I ended up getting about nine off mine. He would probably do better if we both purchased one."

"Perhaps."

"Besides, this way I'd know he doesn't take advantage of you. I can even check the car over, make sure it's decent, if you want to go with a used option, that is."

When I said nothing, Ethan walked right over to a silver SUV and glanced in the window. "What about this one? It would help you deliver all your flowers and such around town. You could even get a decal for the side. Peggy's Petals. You could advertise while you drive around. Plus, it has much more room in it than your current car," he said, smiling and waving for me to come over and look at it.

Instant panic filled me at the thought of giving up my car. I looked at the new vehicle and fought back tears. I couldn't do it. Would the extra space come in handy for delivering flowers, yes? Was my car on the verge of falling apart every time I started it? Yes. Was my car going to cost me a pretty penny to repair? Also, yes. Yet as I stood there in the middle of the lot looking at Ethan, the only thing going through my mind was losing another piece of what I'd once had. Ethan stood there, a smile on his face as he waited for me to come over and look at the SUV he'd decided would be better for me.

"Are you coming? If you don't like this color, we could go with the silver or perhaps the black. We could match." He chuckled.

As he continued talking, anger began building inside of me, followed by frustration, until I couldn't contain it any longer. "I said no, Ethan."

Ethan stopped and spun around, a look of shock on his face. I wasn't good at speaking about my feelings, I knew that, and I realized that from his expression.

"Peggy, I'm sorry."

I didn't want to hear it. "You're sorry? You wouldn't even be able to understand. So please, don't bother trying."

Ethan took a step closer and then stopped. "Well, try

talking to me and maybe I'll be able to," he said, placing his hands on his hips.

I shook my head, turned, and walked back to my car and grabbed the other cup of coffee that sat on the hood. His coffee. He was right behind me as I turned around. I shoved the cup at him and waited while he took it from my hands, and then I pushed him out of the way and got into my car, turning the key.

Ethan approached the window as my car sputtered, failing to turn over. I again turned the key. It continued to sputter, only I didn't quit. I just kept turning it, until finally, it roared to life.

"Peggy, wait a minute. Please talk to me," he pleaded.

"I can't. You wouldn't understand. Trust me."

"I wouldn't understand what? Peggy, please, just calm down and talk to me. No one will understand if you don't communicate."

"Just never mind. Get your truck. I don't need to communicate with you about this. The answer is no." I pulled out of the spot and drove away, leaving Ethan standing alone in the parking lot.

I went through a pile of emotions as I drove back to Willow Valley alone. I'd just turned into my driveway when my actual actions hit me. I cut the engine just in time for my tears to stream down my cheeks. I'd acted in haste over something so stupid, and I'd left Ethan stranded in Cedar Landing. What sort of person was I? I gripped the steering wheel so tight in anger and frustration that my knuckles turned white.

I climbed out of the car, slammed my door, and went inside. Kicking my shoes off, I flopped down on the couch and sobbed. Half an hour later, feeling absolutely exhausted from the outpouring of emotions, I stood in my kitchen pouring hot water into my mug. Tea always calmed me, so I picked up the mug and carried it into the living room, where I sat down in what used to be Darren's chair and took a sip. Then I opened the door to the cabinet under the table. Reaching inside, I pulled out our old green photo album and placed it on my lap.

I sat and stared at the cover. It had been a long time since I'd flipped through the memories of us. Years, to be honest. I reached for the TV remote and turned it on—I needed some sort of background noise—then took another sip of my tea, feeling the warmth inside my body. I placed my mug down, took a deep breath, and opened the book.

I looked down at each of the pictures, flipping slowly from page to page. Wonderful memories flooded my mind, trips to the beach, picnics, fishing, dinner on the pier in Cedar Landing. I smiled as I came to the pictures from the night we'd gotten engaged. We both looked so happy, I thought as my fingers ran over the photograph.

I flipped through the next part of the book, remembering our trip to Vegas right after we'd been married. Then when we finally purchased our home. We both stood out front at the sale sign, grinning like fools, not having any idea what we were getting ourselves into. I looked through all the renovation pictures and home warming parties. Then I flipped to the last page of the book and a tear rolled down my face.

There was a picture of Darren and me, his arms wrapped around me. We stood in front of the car that now sat in my driveway, a large red bow on it. He'd bought it for my birthday. He knew I'd been saving, and it was the car I'd wanted. I'd seen it on the lot two months earlier, but the price was still too high for me. Only I didn't let that stop me. I continued working, picking up extra hours and saving, and had finally saved enough when our washer and dryer broke down. I'd had no choice but to take money from my savings to replace it. Darren had only just started his new job, and we needed his money for other things.

We'd been out shopping for a new light fixture when we drove by the car lot once again on the way home. My eyes zeroed in on what I'd been calling my car for months as we drove by, staying glued to it as we drove on past. A week later, we lay in bed talking.

"Just let me get you the car," he said the night before my birthday. "You've worked so hard."

I shook my head. "No, Darren, you support this household. I want to buy my car," I said as I stared at the dark ceiling of our bedroom.

When I'd told him I wanted my own car, I could see the worry on his face. We were already running tight every month, and I knew he was trying to calculate how we'd afford another insurance payment.

"Stop worrying. I don't want to strain our household finances. I'll save the rest of the money," I said, feeling proud, and that was what I planned to do.

"I know you want to pay for it yourself. You've practically got all the money. I'll just help a little," Darren said. I knew he was still feeling bad about me having to pay for the washer and dryer.

I shook my head. "No. It's fine. I don't mind waiting. It will only take me another month."

"You are one hell of a stubborn woman. You know that."

"I know. That was what made you fall in love with me, remember?" I giggled, rolling over to kiss him good night.

"Being stubborn is cute, but being so stubborn you refuse my help is annoying as hell," he said, kissing me.

The next morning, Darren called me from work and asked me to meet him at Fancy's Restaurant for lunch. I'd gotten a ride with a friend of mine and met Darren at 1. We had lunch, and then he said he had a birthday surprise for me. I frowned as he pulled me across the street and over to the spot where the car I'd been eyeing sat. Only when I saw it, my heart sank. It had been wrapped with a large red bow.

"Oh gosh. It looks like they have sold it," I said to Darren as he grabbed the handle of the driver's side door. "Probably shouldn't touch it."

"You're right," he said, turning and handing me a card.

I took it from his hand and looked down at the envelope. My name was scrawled across the back of it and underneath it read Happy Birthday. I looked at the envelope and then the car and then at Darren. "Tell me you didn't," I cried, not sure if I were happy or upset.

"I did," he said, smiling.

I burst into tears at what he'd just presented to me as he wrapped his arms around me. I wasn't sure if the tears were happy ones or not. Not that I wasn't grateful for the gift he'd just given me. I was. It was more the principal; it was something I'd wanted and promised to do on my own.

"Happy Birthday, my dearest. I hope you enjoy your new wheels."

"God, I hate you." I half laughed, half cried. "Thank you so much."

"Here, we need to get a picture."

As if on cue, my girlfriend, who'd dropped me off and had lunch with us, snapped a picture of us.

I looked down at the picture in the book. Darren stood behind me, his arms wrapped around me. We looked happy as hell, but I could remember that inside I was boiling over with anger.

That anger somehow was still present inside of me today when Ethan was trying to get me to replace the car that Darren had given me. Most people would have looked at that car as the thing that took Darren from me, but I looked at it as the last thing he'd given me.

I closed my eyes as the memory of our argument from that night flooded my mind. If my girlfriend hadn't left, perhaps the fight would have happened at home instead of in the parking lot. Memories of the words I'd screamed at him flooded my mind. I closed the album and shoved it back under the table where it belonged. Leaving my tea, I shut the light off and crawled into bed, praying that tomorrow would be a better day.

Ethan

I rolled over and stared at the clock on the small night table. It was only a little after four in the morning. I'd barely slept again. The conversation between Peggy and I had played over in my mind every time I'd closed my eyes. It had been that way for a few days. I didn't have a clue what had set her off on Sunday, but somehow, I knew I'd missed something. A sign from her. But no matter how many times I played it over in my mind, I couldn't figure it out. The only thing I figured was that it had something to do with her car.

I rolled onto my back and kicked the covers off, slipping out of bed. If I couldn't sleep, there was no point in lying there torturing myself. I made my way into the bathroom and turned the shower on. Once the water heated, I slipped inside and allowed the hot water to run over me.

Once showered, I got dressed and quietly slipped from my room and down the main stairway, careful not to make too much noise, and slipped out the front door. I walked over and sat down on one of the Adirondack chairs that faced the pond.

Daylight had just broken. This was my favourite time of day. I was always up in the early mornings, and I'd grown used to watching the sun rise. It was quiet and a good way to de-stress and spend time with my own thoughts without a lot of outside noise creeping in.

However, this morning was different. There was a lot of noise in my mind, and nothing seemed to quiet it. I'd sat on the porch for over an hour, looking out over the water, and then picked up my book, trying to read a few chapters. When I grew frustrated, I closed it, only to have my mind begin racing again. I could barely sit still any longer and decided to make my way over to my new truck and hop in. I wanted to talk with Peggy, yet I doubted she wanted to speak with me. Besides, she probably wasn't even up yet. I'd left her alone the last couple of days. Even I needed time to process what had happened. But today was her day off.

I wanted to go talk with her, but I also wasn't good with feelings. It appeared now that she wasn't either, and for the two of us to explain things to one another, it would probably only lead to another fight. I'd grown used to not having to explain things to anyone but myself. This was completely unfamiliar territory for me. Instead, I decided I'd go see Melinda. Perhaps she could help me with my problem.

I parked the truck in front of The Crispy Biscuit and made my way inside. It was quiet. Only one other table was full, so I took a seat at one table by the window and waited while Melinda made her way over.

"Hey, Dad," she greeted me as she flipped my cup right-side up and poured me a mug of coffee. "Is Bessy not feeding you enough?"

"Morning," I bit out, not answering her question.

"Uh-oh," Melinda said under her breath as she studied me.

"Uh-oh what?" I questioned. "I'm hungry."

"No, you're not. Something is wrong. I can tell that this calls for a cinnamon bun and some daughter time," she said, flipping over another mug and pouring some coffee into it. "I'll be right back."

I frowned as I watched Melinda cross the floor of the small diner. She whispered something to Cici, who was busy filling up the display cases, and made her way around the counter, where she pulled out two large cinnamon buns. Then she disappeared into the kitchen.

I took a sip of coffee and sat back against the seat, watching out the front window. I was lost in my own thoughts when a plate with a cinnamon bun was set down in front of me and my daughter sat down across from me.

"It was the underwear, wasn't it?" she questioned, running her fingers through her hair.

I frowned, not saying a word.

"We should have gotten you the briefs. I knew Peggy would be a brief woman, not a boxer woman," she said, shaking her head. "Next time, you just need to trust me and go with my gut. If you had mentioned you may go all the way, I would have insisted."

"Please, just stop. This has nothing to do with underwear. Besides, the goings on in my bedroom are none of your concern. Let's get that straight right now."

Her cheeks reddened. "Got it."

I watched my daughter, her eyes falling to the plate in front of her. "Sorry," I bit out. "I know you're only trying to help."

"Dad, what is it? I mean, you look... devastated." Melinda took a bite of the cinnamon bun and licked the icing from her lips.

"I messed up."

"Again?"

I looked at my daughter and shook my head. Did she think getting to know someone was easy? It was for kids their age; they had the internet. Dating apps. Hell, I heard some things the guys did while away on leave. Most things I wouldn't have done with my wife. It was almost as if their actions didn't have consequences. "Yes, again. This dating business is for the birds."

"What happened? You weren't really going on a date. You were going car shopping."

"Yes, to us old people, that could be considered a date."

Melinda smiled at me. "Okay so, what did you do?"

I shrugged. "Beats the hell out of me. Peggy told me about her car in her letters, that it needed repairs. She mentioned she may need a new one even. When I picked her up the other night, she told me it was making a horrible noise, and when we drove out yesterday, I heard it. I knew just by looking at it, she was right to think she needed a new one. So, I mentioned it to her while we were shopping yesterday that perhaps we could find her a car while there, perhaps get a package deal, and she blew up on me."

Melinda flinched. A knowing look came over her face as she nodded her head. "I see."

"You see what?"

Melinda was quiet for a moment. I could tell she was holding something back from me. I wasn't certain what it was, but I wanted to know.

"Are you going to sit there looking like you're holding onto the world's biggest secret, or are you going to talk to your old man and tell him what it is he's done? I mean, all I did was care."

"Oh, Dad. It's really not my place, but just know you didn't really do anything wrong. It's more the subject of what you were suggesting that caused the issue."

I looked at my daughter with confusion. What did she mean by that? I cleared my throat. "I'm asking you, aren't I? Peggy sure as hell won't tell me. She's probably never going to speak to me again, and here you are speaking in some sort of woman code."

Melinda laughed. "Oh, Dad. Peggy isn't like that. It's just, I'm not the right person to ask. I don't want to get something wrong. If you want to find out, and don't want to ask Peggy, then I suggest you ask Trinity. She is, after all, her best friend."

"As in bookstore Trinity?"

Melinda nodded. "I'm sure she will be in here any minute. She and Peggy normally meet up on Tuesday mornings for breakfast. Although they are rather late this morning," she said, looking at her watch. "Perhaps they aren't meeting today. It's rare, but sometimes happens."

"I don't know if it's a good idea that she sees me here," I said, shoving the rest of the bun into my mouth.

"Dad, seriously, Peggy really isn't like that. I'd be shocked if she wouldn't speak to you. Just wait and see what happens."

I'd taken Melinda's advice and waited at The Crispy Biscuit, but by the time 10 rolled around, I'd given up hope that either of them would come in. Instead, I paid my bill and drove down to the bookstore. It pleasantly surprised me to find the place empty. It would make having this conversation a little easier. I didn't want to be talking in front of others about such a private matter. Trinity was working behind the counter when I entered. The little bells jingled as I walked in.

Trinity looked up from the book she was reading, a smile spreading across her face. "Hey, Ethan."

"Hey. Good morning."

"Morning. Beautiful day out today. What can I help you find today?" she asked, placing her book on the counter. "Thomas just finished another one of those political thrillers you like."

I said nothing. I felt completely out of place just asking her about the situation with Peggy. Instead, I glanced over to the shelf of true crime, about to ask her if she carried a certain author, when she cleared her throat.

"It's okay, Ethan. I can see you're uncomfortable. I was only trying to break the ice a bit." She smiled. "Melinda already called. Why don't you take a seat?" she said, nodding to one of the large wingback chairs.

Before I could sit down, she'd already come around the counter, picked up the cat that slept on one of the seats of the chairs, and sat down, waiting for me to join her.

"So, Melinda filled me in about the car lot."

Thank goodness for my kid, I thought to myself as I shifted uncomfortably in my seat. "Can you tell me what I did?" I questioned, feeling completely confused. I hoped that just by jumping in and asking, I'd grow more comfortable talking with her.

Trinity softly smiled and shook her head. "You did nothing. I'm guessing Peggy never told you what exactly happened to Darren, did she?"

"Well, I know he passed away. Other than that, she stays tight-lipped about him, even in her letters. To be honest, I think she only mentioned him once or twice, and when I tried to get her to tell me about him the other night, she just kept changing the subject."

Trinity nodded. "Yes, Peggy rarely speaks of him. I think I may be the one and only person she's told in this entire town, to be honest."

I frowned, unsure if I really wanted to know the truth now, if it was that bad.

"Peggy doesn't talk about it, and honestly, I'm not sure I should even tell you, but I love my friend, and I know that somewhere deep inside, she really likes you. I'd never seen her so happy in the months that you were writing to one another. She'd never admit that either, just so you know," Trinity said, giving me a gentle smile.

"She isn't an easy person to get to know, is she?"

"Oh, I wouldn't say that. I prefer to say that... she's guarded."

"That's a good way of putting it." I nodded. I was feeling more comfortable talking to her now that Melinda had already broken the ice for me. I felt that if I came in questioning you about Peggy, Trinity may send me on my way and call her, blowing my chances with her.

"Peggy's husband died in a car accident."

"Yes, she mentioned an accident. I don't think it's that big of a deal. Many people do." I shrugged, not quite understanding what the actual issue was.

Trinity nodded. "That is true, but it's not about how it happened. It's about what happened leading up to that accident. They were at a local car lot."

"Whoa, wait a minute. A local lot in Cedar Landing?"

Trinity nodded. "Yes. That is where Peggy and Darren used to live."

"Let me guess. Was it the large lot on the right-hand side of the road. The one that is clearly the largest but the one she didn't want to go to?" I questioned.

"Yes. She'd been saving for a car, and Darren bought her a car instead of her waiting until she finished saving for it."

"Okay," I replied, "I don't understand why that would bother her."

"To understand that, you need to know that Peggy is very independent. She works hard, and when she has her mind set on something, it's best not to get in her way. Take that as a snippet of free advice and put it in your back pocket." Trinity winked. "Anyway, he'd surprised her with it on her birthday. He'd had one of her friends bring her down to the lot, and she'd figured the car had sold when he brought her over to it. They'd wrapped it in a large red ribbon, and that's when he surprised her. Anyway, while her friend was there, everything was fine. It was after she left things got out of hand."

"What do you mean?"

"Well, she'd been saving, and she'd really wanted to purchase this car on her own. Finances were tight, and she knew that the added expense on insurance could strain them. You see, Darren paid for everything around the house. He never wanted her to have to pay for things. The money she worked for was hers to do as she wanted. She didn't want Darren stressing over an added expense, so that was why she was hell-bent on saving the entire amount to purchase the car.

"Anyway, she told him she'd go to the bank and get the money she'd saved and give it to him. Of course, with this being a gift, he wouldn't hear of it. He told her to keep it. No matter how much she persisted, he refused, until they were in a full-blown argument. Words were said, many actually, and Peggy stormed off the lot in the new car, leaving Darren behind to follow her."

"I see."

"She drove home, and once she calmed down, she got dinner on, knowing that Darren had probably taken some time to cool off before coming home. Peggy wanted to apologize to him, so she made his favorite meal. Once dinner had finished cooking, she waited a bit and then finally ate and put his meal in the fridge. She thought perhaps he was hurting too badly to come home. She went to bed angrier than she'd been when she got home. Instead, she figured she would apologize in the morning when all emotions had simmered down."

I sat there waiting patiently for her to continue.

Trinity looked at me, sadness in her eyes. "Anyway, in the wee hours of the morning, Peggy woke up to a large thud. She got up out of bed and looked out of the bedroom door for Darren. Only the house was dark and empty. She heard another thud and realized that it was someone knocking on the front door. Worried that it was an emergency, she ran to the door and answered it. That was when she came face-to-face with two police officers who notified her that Darren had been killed in an accident."

"What? Are you serious?" I said, closing my eyes, trying to imagine what that must have been like. How her world had shattered in a heartbeat.

"Apparently, after she left the lot, Darren took a few minutes to calm down before getting behind the wheel. When he did, he took the long way home, which involved a few extremely bad blind curves. He apparently went to go around a car that had stalled on the worst blind curve in Cedar Landing and met a car head-on. The driver of the other car was drunk. He survived, but Darren died instantly."

I sat there for a minute, going over what Trinity had told me. "Trinity, call me insensitive, but I still don't really understand what I did? All I did was suggest that it was time for her to get a new car."

Trinity nodded her head and met my eyes. "The car, the one she drives today, is the car that Darren bought for her. It's literally the last piece of him she has left."

I nodded. "That, combined with the fact that she never had a chance to apologize, is probably consuming her."

"No doubt," Trinity answered. "I also think that perhaps she feels that by keeping the car, it is her way of apologizing, which may sound completely stupid, but in ways I can somehow understand that."

I thought about it; she was right. "That makes sense. I just thought I was helping."

"There is no way you could have possibly known. I think the wound is still deep. I know that she's been having a hard time this year as well. Harder than the past ones. It may be because she feels it's time to move on and let herself date again. Don't punish yourself too much, Ethan. Peggy is a wonderful woman with a very delicate heart, and one worth getting to know. She just has a few demons that she needs to work out."

"I know that. I can't tell you how much I like her

already, and that is just from getting to know her through her letters. I know she is a special woman. Perhaps I'll head over there tomorrow. For now, I need to figure out how to approach her."

Trinity smiled. "Approach her the same way you have been. If she communicates best through a letter, write her an email. She will eventually open up to you. Somewhere inside of her, even if she is fighting it, she really likes Ethan Alexander. I know my friend. It may take her time to show that to you, but she will."

I felt better after speaking with Trinity, and once I returned to the inn, I did exactly as she had suggested. I sat down and wrote one long-ass email to Peggy. Now I just needed to wait for a reply.

Thursday, I pulled up out front of Peggy's Petals to find the flower shop dark and the closed sign dangling in the window. I glanced at the clock; shortly after 6. I frowned. I was sure she was open until 8. It had been two days since I'd emailed her, and I still hadn't gotten a response. I couldn't wait any longer, so I drove down here. Climbing out of the truck, I stepped up to the window, finally seeing her posted hours there. I was right...she was supposed to close at 8.

The first thought that came into my mind was that she was sick, so I made my way over to her place. I pulled up along the opposite side of the street and looked over to her driveway. Her car was there, and I could see a light on in the front window. Perhaps I was right, and she was sick. Worried, I climbed out of the car and headed to her door.

I placed my foot on the bottom step of her small porch only to have it break under my weight. "Fuck," I muttered to myself, as I made a mental note to come back and fix that.

I made my way to the door and took a minute, then raised my hand and knocked. A minute later, Peggy stood in front of me. I could tell by her expression that she was curious as to why I was here.

"Could I come in?" I questioned.

Her eyes wandered over me and without a word, she took a step back, giving me room to come in. She closed the door behind me then made her way toward her small kitchen.

I removed my shoes and followed her. "Peggy, I wanted to apologize," I blurted out, not wanting another moment to go by without telling her that.

She shook her head. "Ethan, you have nothing to apologize for. It's me who must apologize to you. I overreacted."

I watched as she picked up a screwdriver and began removing the screws to the hinges on her kitchen cupboard doors.

"That may be, but I also need to apologize." She looked at me. "I didn't know."

She nodded, then put her focus on the task at hand, turning her back to me. "I take it Trinity told you?"

"She did. Don't be angry with her. I sent you an—"

"I got it," Peggy grumbled as she struggled with the screwdriver. Finally, she moved from the one hinge she'd been working on to another one. I could see the frustration on her face as she struggled once again with that screw.

"Renovating?" I questioned.

"Trying." she said, her voice shaking with frustration.

I could tell she was getting upset as she continued to work at removing the hinges that were probably so seized it would take a drill to remove them.

"Dammit," she muttered under her breath. "They are in there so tight; this is going to be impossible."

I walked over, stepped up behind her, and placed my hand over hers. "Let me," I murmured.

It surprised me she didn't fight me. Instead, she leaned her body back against mine and let go of the screwdriver. She stayed there, while I removed the first screw with what looked like ease, and that was when I felt her body begin to shake.

I put the screwdriver down on the counter and placed my hands on her shoulders. The second I touched her, she buried her face in her hands and sobbed. "Everything is just so hard," she cried.

I didn't know exactly what I was supposed to do. I just stood there for a moment, my hands on her shoulders, attempting to comfort her. Then I wondered if I should step away. I didn't know. I hadn't done this in so long, I felt like I was playing a guessing game. But she made my decision easy for me. She spun around and wrapped her arms around me, crying into my chest.

"Everything is just falling apart," she cried. "Me included."

"Not everything," I said, my voice low as I wrapped my arms around her, embracing her.

"All I wanted to do was refinish the cupboards," she muttered. "Just update them a little."

Once she stopped crying and, with her still in my arms, I brought my forefinger to her chin and lightly tilted her head so her eyes could meet mine. Her blue eyes, glassy from the tears, showed me just how vulnerable she was in this moment. I'd felt like I'd gotten to know her well through our letters, only to find out that she'd hidden this part—the part that housed her emotions. If I thought she was beautiful before from the things I already knew, this was the icing on the cake. I loved strong women, but I also loved them when they weren't afraid to show this side of themselves.

We stood there, our eyes locked, not a word passing between us. As I stared down into her eyes, I slowly leaned forward and allowed my lips to graze over hers. When she didn't jump back, I kissed her again, this time with a little more pressure. I felt her body slowly relax as her arms wrapped around my neck, her fingers running through the hair on the back of my head.

"I'm sorry," she whispered, our lips parting as she now sat up on the kitchen counter where I'd put her. "I wanted to write you back. I just needed to get over this moment of weakness."

"Never be sorry for showing me, or anyone else, how you feel," I said, my forehead resting against hers. "As for writing me back, well, I'll forgive you. I have waited much longer for your letters."

Looking deep into my eyes, she softly smiled. "That sounds funny coming from a strong man like you. Someone who has admitted that they don't show their feelings very well, either."

I shrugged. "Let's say I'm learning to do that as well."

"Oh." Her eyes didn't leave mine as she brought her hand to my cheek. "How about we learn this together?" she whispered.

I swallowed hard at the look in her eyes and nodded, resting my forehead against hers.

It was then that she brought her lips to mine for the first time, then she wrapped her arms around my neck. Wrapping my arms around her, I slid her forward on the counter, her legs resting on either side of my hips, and I pulled her in tight to me, attempting to continue comforting her.

Peggy

Four Weeks Later

I helped Trisha and Sarah load the last pile of things into Carl's van. I stood back, hands on hips as I ran through a mental checklist, making sure that we weren't forgetting anything. Today was the day of the summer festival. The day where most of the small businesses and other crafters in Willow Valley moved to the outdoors in the park and sold goods to the floods of tourists that drove through. The organizers had offered me a table for free that I'd originally turned down. After a long conversation with Ethan and Trinity, I decided that I really needed to be present to represent Peggy's Petals and asked once again for the table.

"You girls sure you are going to be okay without me there?" I questioned.

Both Trisha and Sarah smiled. "Of course. Besides, you will be there, just not actively working. We will know where to find you if we need you."

"Did you grab the table wrap and the canopy from inside?" I questioned as they climbed into the van Sarah had borrowed from her mom.

"It was the very first thing we put in."

"You know where the booth is, right?"

"Yep, beside Bluebird Books. Ava is running that table for Trinity."

"Okay, you sure you have everything? I just feel as if you are forgetting something," I said, fidgeting, looking at all the boxes inside the back of the van.

"Have fun, girls," Ethan said as he stepped up beside me, placing his large hand on the small of my back. "I'll keep Peggy busy while you two look after things." He winked.

"By, Mr. Alexander," they said in unison as they giggled. I waved and watched as they pulled away from the curb, leaving Ethan and me standing there.

"You just about ready?" he asked, looking me over.

I smiled and looked down at myself. I was still in my yoga pants and an old concert T-shirt. I'd pulled my hair back in a messy bun when I'd gotten up and had come right outside to help the girls load things up. "Um...not really," I said, crinkling my nose at him. "I still need to shower."

"Have you had breakfast?"

I shook my head. "No."

Ethan smiled. "I figured I'd best get over here. I knew you'd be worried about today. Come, I'll put on some coffee and make us some breakfast, while you take your time showering and getting ready," he said, guiding me gently toward the front of my house.

"So, Ethan, have you decided about staying in Willow Valley yet?" Thomas questioned.

The four of us sat on a blanket underneath two large willow trees, a plate of fries still in front of us. It was the only place we'd found out of the way of the crowds where the four of us could have lunch.

Over the past four weeks, Ethan and I had grown closer than I'd thought possible. While he still had his room at the Willow Valley Bed and Breakfast, he had spent a few nights at my place on my couch. It had become a normal occurrence, especially after he spent the day helping me with some chores around the house that I wasn't able to do myself.

"I have. I've decided this is where I'd like to settle down."

"I think we are going to look next week for a place for Ethan." I leaned forward and grabbed a couple of fries from the plate in front of us.

"That's wonderful," Trinity said. "Melinda must be very excited that you've decided to stay as well."

"She is. She's been asking since I arrived. Couldn't keep stringing her along much longer."

Thomas smiled. "Well, you know, Peggy keeps telling me how good you are with carpentry after she saw Peggy's kitchen cupboard that you worked on. If you are interested, I can always use some help at the shop. I mean, after you get settled into your new place, that is."

"That would be great. It will keep me busy. As soon as I get settled into a place, then count me in," Ethan replied.

Ethan and Thomas had developed quite a friendship over the past four weeks as well. We'd shared numerous dinners together and had gone on a couple of day trips together. Trinity and I were glad of that; they'd even started joining us a morning a month for our Tuesday morning breakfast meetups.

"So, have you started looking at any places?" Trinity asked.

Ethan looked over at me and placed his hand on my upper leg. I nodded. "I grabbed a couple real estate magazines at The Crispy Biscuit the other day. We went through them last night. There were a few places Ethan was interested in. But to go and see them, no."

Trinity cleared her throat after taking a sip of her pop. "You know, I heard that the little cottage out on Willow Valley Bay is finally for sale. I don't know if they listed it publicly yet, but you really should go out and peek at that place. It's old, and may even need some work, but I remember dreaming of living there when I was a kid."

"I never saw it listed," I said, looking at Ethan, who was shaking his head. I was pretty sure I knew the place Trinity was talking about. "It's that cottage style home, isn't it? It's been empty for a while now?"

"Yes, that is the one." Trinity nodded.

"It sounds like something I would like. I love to spend my mornings looking out over the small pond behind the bed and breakfast. It's so soothing."

"Thomas, didn't you tell me you thought Serenity had the listing?" Trinity questioned.

Thomas nodded. "I'm sure that is what I heard. Joe was the one who told me, I'm almost sure of it. Check with Serenity. I know that place will go fast if it hits the market. It was one of the most sought-after places out here when we were growing up."

Ethan wrapped his arms around me and pulled me back between his legs. "I guess we will talk to Serenity," he whispered into my ear.

"I guess we will."

We'd finished the plate of fries when we noticed Brooke and Tristan walking across the field toward us, carrying a plate of something, along with a tray of coffee.

"There you guys are," she said, placing the plate down on the ground. "Thought I would bring over some of those lemon blueberry scones you love before they are all gone."

"Oh, my dear, you are a lifesaver," I said, lifting the cover and taking out a scone.

"Good turnout this year. The flowers look amazing as well, Peggy." Tristan smiled, sitting down on the ground, grabbing a scone and coffee.

"Um, what do you think you are doing?" Brooke questioned, her hands on her hips as she looked down at Tristan.

"Taking a much-deserved break. Exactly what you should be doing." He winked, then grinned at all of us. "Melinda and Cici have the table. You can sit down for five minutes."

The five of us laughed as Brooke shook her head and sat down on Tristan's lap, joining us. "So, what are we talking about?" Brooke asked.

"About the small cottage on Willow Valley Bay," Ethan said, taking a bite of my scone.

"Ah, yes, it just went up for sale. Serenity was telling me about it the other day," Brooke said. "If only I didn't have the bakery right in my front yard, I'd move there in a heartbeat. I'm sure it will go fast."

Serenity Johnson stood out front of the cottage-style home and handed us the fact sheet. "Word sure spreads fast in this town. Here the Connor's didn't think they'd be able to sell this property."

"If you don't mind me asking, why are the owners selling?" I questioned, looking down at the fact sheet in Ethan's hand. "Is there something wrong with the house?"

"Quite the opposite. They have well maintained the home over the years. It's been in the Connor family for many generations."

"I see. Why don't I recognize the name Connor from here?" I questioned.

"Well, Peggy, you probably wouldn't. The Connor's who lived here passed away about two years before you moved here. The couple who owns it live in Pine Harbour, five hours north of here. Tim and Verena Connor are the parents of Ella Darling."

A shiver ran through me. Ella had passed away a

couple of years ago. "Ah, well, it's a shame that they are selling it as opposed to leaving it for Connor."

"It is, but Connor needs to build a new barn after the last storm that passed through. He also needs to do some other upgrades to some equipment. Plus, the old farmhouse needs some repairs. Unfortunately, it all comes with a hefty price tag. Word around town is that the bank has denied him any more loan money. So, Tim and Verena came to me and wanted to sell the place and surprise him with the money from the sale of the cottage. Now, you both didn't hear that from me...and on that note, that is enough gossip on my part." Serenity smiled.

Ethan met my eyes. I could only imagine what was going through his mind as Serenity stood there, spilling all about Connor Darling's problems. Everyone knew Serenity was prone to gossip. Somehow, she seemed to know all the details of everyone's life in Willow Valley. Suddenly, I wondered what sort of rumors she would spread around town about us at this point. I softly smiled at him and nodded toward the fact sheet, pretending to be interested in something on there while Serenity slid the key in the lock.

"Honestly, I think you will really like this property. It sits on a little over an acre, and the water's edge over there is the edge of Willow Valley Bay," she said, pointing to the water. "I will let you know now that I have had more inquiries on this property since opening my agency than any other property in Willow Valley. Even people just passing through during summer vacation have stopped in to inquire. So, if you are even the least bit interested, you'd be best to at least make an offer. Once it hits the real estate booklet in a couple of days, I can assure you it will be gone. Especially at the price they are asking."

Ethan looked over and smiled. "Noted. So, the property butts onto the water?"

"It does."

"So that means I could make a viewing area over the water?"

"I see no reason you couldn't. You'd own the property right up to the water's edge," she said, smiling.

"And I have full access to the lake?"

"You do. The only thing Willow Valley requires is a license to fish and a license to place an ice fishing hut on the lake. Otherwise, you can boat or canoe all you'd like. Would you like to go inside and see the house?"

Ethan nodded and took my hand in his. "Love to."

"Follow me. Unless, of course, you'd like privacy and prefer to go through it on your own."

Not wanting Serenity to hang on to our every word, I smiled. "We can look, and we will make a list of any questions we have."

"Sure thing." She nodded, pushing the door open.

"I think this would be perfect," he whispered into my

ear as we stepped through the door. "I mean, being close to the lake every morning would make my day."

I smiled as we stepped inside. Ethan glanced down at the fact sheet. "Says here that everything has been recently renovated. The kitchen and all bathrooms, freshly painted bedrooms and new hardwood floors and carpets throughout. That's a bonus."

"It is," I said as I ran my hand over the quartz countertop as Ethan followed behind me. "It's beautiful," I agreed, opening the pantry cupboard to check for storage. "Would you look at this pantry? Goodness, you could probably fit the entire pantry at The Crispy Biscuit in here." I giggled.

Ethan stepped up behind me and looked inside the pantry as well. "It's perfect," he replied as we continued through the rest of the house. We checked out the family room, which looked out over the lake, then into the master bedroom, which also had a view of the lake. They had renovated the master ensuite to include a large two-person shower along with a large soaker tub. The last two bedrooms were smaller but still larger than we expected, and they shared another three-piece bathroom.

"This really would be perfect," Ethan responded as we headed back to the kitchen to meet up with Serenity out front.

"Well, what did you want to do? Did you want to see the other places first?"

Ethan looked around the kitchen and then shook his head. "No, I think this is the one."

"All right then." I smiled. "Let's talk to Serenity."

"Well?" she asked as we stepped out the front door hand in hand.

"I think it's perfect," Ethan replied.

"Wonderful. So, it's probably best if you make an offer if you are serious. We can see if they accept it and, in the meantime, we can always look at the other places you wanted to see."

Ethan looked at me and then nodded. "I am going to put in an offer. No need to look at the others," he said, his voice exuding confidence.

"All right then, meet me at the office and we will get to it," she said, locking the front door behind her.

Ethan

I shut up the back of my truck and locked it, then glanced at my watch. It was a little after 1. I'd come to Cedar Landing today to pick some things up for Peggy's shop and had called Melinda to see if she wanted to join me for some furniture shopping. I'd found out earlier in the week that they had accepted my offer on the house, and I already had a closing date. Plus, I wanted to talk to Melinda about something and I figured today was a perfect day to do it.

"We should just about be ready to go and furniture shop," I said as Melinda made her way back from a coffee shop across the street.

"Perfect. I grabbed you a black coffee," she said, waving the to-go cup in the air.

"Great. I'm going to need it." I chucked. I knew how

picky Melinda was with clothes, so I could only imagine she was the same or worse with furniture.

"Oh, Dad. It will not be that bad."

"Judging from how picky you are with clothes, I think it will probably be unbearable."

Melinda let out a laugh and climbed into the front of my truck.

"This is all, Mr. Alexander," the young man who had been helping load up my truck said, plopping the last box in the back of my truck. "Just be careful. This one is fragile."

"Do I need to sign anything?" I questioned.

"Oh yeah, one minute, and I'll get those directions for you too."

With the form signed, my truck loaded, and directions in hand, Melinda and I made our way to the furniture store across town.

"So, Dad, what do you think you'll need?" she questioned, looking at the first dining room set we came to.

"Well, to be honest, I'm going to need everything." I shrugged. "I sold everything before I left, aside from what I gave to you."

"Everything? Dad, you must have something?"

"No, I need everything. Hope you're ready to pick out some things."

Melinda took a seat at a table, pulling out a notepad and pen from her purse. She clicked the pen twice, then looked up at me. "All right. Just tell me what you need or the rooms you have, the style you'd like, and I'll make a list and we will go from there."

Shopping turned out to be easier than I thought it would be. Between Melinda and the sales associate at the store, I had a completely furnished home. It felt good to have that weight off my shoulders.

"Did you want to grab a quick bite with your old man?" I questioned as we drove down the main street of Cedar Landing, back toward Willow Valley.

"Sure, we could try that little fish and chip hut we passed on the way in if you like. I've heard they have great food, and I've always wanted to try it. I don't normally get out this way too much."

"Sounds good," I replied, turning into the parking lot that held the little fish and chip hut.

Once we got our food, we took a seat at a small picnic table that was placed under a tree at the edge of the parking lot. The pair of us opened our cans of soda at the same time and took a sip.

"Things going better now with Peggy?" Melinda asked.

It was as if she knew. "I actually wanted to speak to you about something that involves Peggy," I said as Melinda dipped a fry into the small container of ketchup.

"Oh."

"I want to know how you feel about her?"

Melinda looked at me and shrugged. "I've told you, Peggy is a wonderful lady. Why do you ask? Is it not working out?"

I chuckled. "Quite the opposite. For the past month or so, I've been helping her with some renovations at her place. It's really run-down."

"Yeah, it is. I'm sure it needs a lot of work."

"Well, I just bought the house, and I wanted to see how you felt about her because I've been thinking of asking her to move in with me."

Melinda paused, her fork halfway up to her mouth. "Whoa, Dad, that's...that's awesome." Melinda shoved two fries into her mouth. "Have you mentioned it to her yet?"

I shook my head. "No. I was planning to talk to her this weekend about it but wanted to see what you thought of the idea first. If you thought it was stupid, well, then I'd just pass on it."

"Why would I think it was stupid?"

I said nothing. I just looked at my daughter. She was right. Why was it stupid?

"Dad, if you really like Peggy and are serious about being with her, then I think you should go for it. A wise man once told me to swing for the fences in everything I do. I have made some of my best decisions based on that advice."

I smiled. I remembered telling her that. "Way to use my own words against me there, kid."

Melinda laughed. "I say go for it."

We took our time eating lunch and when we were finished, we headed back into Willow Valley. I pulled the truck up out front of Peggy's Petals and hoped out, Melinda joining me. "Where does Peggy want all this stuff?" she questioned.

"I'm not sure. I'll go inside and see."

I had almost made it to the door when Peggy stepped outside, smiling. "Hey, Melinda. Ethan. How did it go?" she asked, placing a kiss on my cheek.

I wrapped my arm around her, and together we walked over to the back of my truck. "Well, they gave me everything that came in. It looked like it was everything on the list," I said, opening the tailgate to show her all the boxes.

"Oh, amazing."

"What all did you order, Peggy?" Melinda asked, coming over beside us.

"Oh, some different vases, mug vases, and a bunch of others. Probably too many options, to be honest. I also ordered a few spa type items for birthdays and anniversaries to add to my inventory. I've had an increase in requests for those things."

"Ohhh, really. Fantastic. I will have to tell Tristan. I

know he was asking me the other day some ideas on what to get for Brooke for their upcoming year anniversary."

"Isn't it a little early?"

"Yes." Melinda laughed. "He told me he likes to be well-prepared." The three of us laughed. "I'd love to see the spa type items myself."

"Sure thing," Peggy said, grabbing one box.

"All right, so where do you want this stuff?" I questioned, watching her walk away from me.

"Um, just bring it inside and stack it in the corner. I'll get it put away."

"Okay. Melinda, grab a box or two."

Together, we had the truck unloaded in ten minutes and the boxes stacked inside the small entryway of the store. I'd just returned from the bathroom and found Peggy showing Melinda one of the spa kits.

"I'm going to run Melinda home and I'll be back to help you with all this stuff," I said, leaning in and placing a kiss on her cheek, while she went back to working on an arrangement.

"Okay, oh, and I thought I'd have you over for dinner tomorrow. To celebrate the new home." Peggy looked at me, smiling.

"I'd love that."

Peggy

I stirred the sugar into my coffee as I sat across from Trinity, listening to her complain about how much Thomas had been working over the past couple of months.

"I barely see him anymore, between the store and all the orders he'd been getting."

I couldn't help but smile. "You know, not that long ago you could barely stand the sight of the man, and now here you are, complaining you never see him. How times have changed."

Trinity looked at me. "Okay there, pot."

"Oh no, don't you dare bring me into this."

"Why not? You didn't even want to write a letter to a stranger, and now here you are in a relationship with one." Trinity laughed, sticking her tongue out at me. "A relationship that I'm thinking is starting to get pretty serious."

It was true. Ethan and I had gone from strangers to having our first fight to now being practically inseparable. We spent most evenings and weekends and my days off together. Recently, he'd even started coming into the shop, repairing a few things here and there and doing some work that I was having a hard time getting done.

"I'll just be happy once Ethan can start giving him a hand. He comes home at night exhausted. It would be nice to not have him fall asleep while eating dinner."

I smiled. "Speaking of dinner, Ethan is coming by tonight. We are celebrating the close of the house."

"What are you making?"

"Hmm, I was thinking chicken. I have a few recipes picked out."

"Wonderful. Do you have enough for a third?" Trinity laughed.

"You know I love you, but..." I could feel the blush rise to my cheeks in wanting to be alone with Ethan. I'd never admit it out loud yet. I could barely admit it to myself.

"Uh-huh." Trinity laughed. "Say no more. I can see it all over your face."

I looked at my best friend and shook my head. "No, you can't."

"Peggy, believe what you want, but I can. You love him."

"Back to dinner," I said, trying hard to change the subject before I not only had to admit what I'd been feeling to myself, but out loud to my best friend.

"Deny it all you want. Just know that I can see it." She winked.

I grabbed my lemon blueberry scone off my plate and shoved a piece into my mouth. It was pointless to hide this from Trinity longer, just like she hadn't been able to hide her feelings for Thomas from me.

Ethan stood at the counter, seasoning the chicken for the barbeque. I watched from the corner of my eye while he worked. I'd invited him for dinner, and while I'd gotten off work late and had nothing prepared when he got here, he offered to jump right in and help.

"Where did you learn how to cook?" I questioned while I worked at getting the cork out of the bottle of wine.

Ethan chuckled. "I've been single a long time, and when you tire of the provided meals in the military, you take matters into your own hands. Plus, relationships are give and take. I never ever minded helping in the kitchen or around the house, nor do I now."

Finally, the cork came loose, and I poured the wine into the two glasses that sat in front of me.

"So, we ordered most of the furniture for the new place. I think you'll be happy with Melinda's choices. She really set into the cottage feel and made selections to complement the mood of the house."

"Wonderful. I can't wait to see everything. When does it arrive?"

"Well, it should be there in time for the day I move in. I called Serenity, and she said that if it arrives before everything closes, they are more than willing to allow me access to the house to unload the furniture. It took a bit of pressure off. I just need to let Serenity know."

"That's great. I am so happy for you. It really looks like an amazing house. I will say I am a little jealous of the kitchen."

Ethan smirked. "You can use the kitchen anytime you want."

I could feel Ethan watching me as the words left his lips, but I couldn't seem to meet his eyes.

"Did you hear me?" he questioned, reaching for the bag of potatoes that sat on the counter.

"I did," I answered, still not looking at him. I put the wine bottle back in the fridge and then placed his glass down in front of him.

"Why aren't you saying anything else, and why aren't you looking at me?" Ethan questioned.

Ethan had learned very quickly that when I didn't reply or look his way after he said something that he'd made me uncomfortable. He'd been working on trying to get me to be more open, but instead, I picked up my wine and took a sip then slowly brought my eyes to his. "I don't want to impose," I answered, averting my gaze from his.

"I see. And you think by me offering you the use of my kitchen, you'd be imposing?"

I shrugged my shoulders, still not looking at him.

"Peggy, look at me?"

I took a sip of wine before placing my glass down on the counter and then looked at Ethan. The room grew quiet as we stood there looking at one another. The intensity of his gaze caused my cheeks to heat, and the longer his gaze lingered, the more uncomfortable I became. I could feel the heat from his body as he stepped in closer, closing the space between us.

Placing one hand on my hip and the other under my chin, he tilted my head back. "I mean what I say. You're not an imposition, and I'd love nothing more than to have you use my kitchen whenever the hell you want."

Before I could protest, he leaned in and took my mouth with his in a demanding kiss. In seconds, I practically melted into his arms. His kiss made me forget what I'd said and thought about myself in seconds. He'd consumed me, and I could no longer fight the feelings I had for this man. With my eyes closed, I felt his hands on my body, the embrace of his arms, and the tenderness in his kiss.

When our lips parted, I softly smiled at him, and as his hands released me, my body began silently screaming for them to return.

I gathered the dirty dishes from the small table in my kitchen, leaving a few items behind, and carried them over to the counter. I turned to go back and get the rest only to find Ethan behind me, his hands full.

"Oh, you don't have to do that," I said.

Ethan looked at me and shook his head. "I do. I ate as well, and I don't mind helping."

"Okay." I smiled, turning my back toward him to put the kettle on to make coffee.

I'd just pulled the French press out of the cupboard and placed it on the counter when I felt his arms slide around my waist. He pulled me back against him, kissing my neck. "Dinner was delicious," he murmured.

I closed my eyes and brought my hand up, placing it on the back of his neck as he continued to nip at my neck.

I could feel my body awaken as his hands found their home at the front of my jeans, his rough fingers grazing my bare skin as my shirt lifted.

He brought his hand to my cheek and turned my head, bringing his lips to mine. Closing my eyes, I allowed myself, and my body, to get lost in his kiss. When our lips parted, he spun me around in his arms, pulling me against him.

"I should go," he whispered, his lips on mine.

I nodded as his tongue washed through my mouth, yet neither of us moved. We didn't even hear the kettle scream, signaling that water had boiled.

Ethan

Kissing her, having her arms wrapped around me, was right where I wanted to be.

"I should go," I repeated as she pulled at my shirt, lifting it up over my head and dropping it to the floor. Her eyes said it all—full of want, full of need—which made it impossible for me to leave.

Her eyes dropped to my chest, and she brought her hand up and ran her fingers over the words I'd had tattooed on me years ago. *Brothers in Arms, Strength, Respect, Loyalty.* She kept tracing her fingers over the lettering and then brought her eyes back to mine.

"I like this," she muttered, leaning forward and placing a kiss on my peck, which sent a bolt of electricity through my body.

Placing my hand on her cheek, I crashed into her lips,

devouring her mouth. I picked her up and placed her on the island in the middle of her kitchen, kissing her neck as I slid myself between her legs. God, I wanted to be inside of her. Her scent was intoxicating, and each little whimper she delivered as I placed yet another kiss on her neck went right through me.

"Peggy, I should go," I whispered again, breathing hard. I was worried this was too soon and that she wasn't ready for us to take this step. The last thing I wanted was for her to run from me after this.

"Stay," she whimpered as I sucked her earlobe between my lips.

Arousal flooded me, and I cupped her cheek and looked down at her. At some point, she'd unbuttoned her shirt. It hung open just enough for me to get a peek at the black bra she wore. My cock was already hard just from kissing her. Now knowing she had been quietly unwrapping herself, I was so hard it hurt.

I bit my lower lip as she leaned back on the island, her shirt still covering everything, showing me just enough to tease me. My eyes wandered her body as her shirt fell open, baring her flat stomach. I met her eyes, and then I bent down and placed a kiss right above the button on her jeans. The second my lips connected with her warm, soft skin; she sucked in a breath.

I could tell she wanted more from the look in her eyes. I placed a hand behind her back and reached up with the other, pushing her shirt away, exposing her covered breast to me. I cupped it in my hand and gently squeezed as my lips met her silky skin again.

"Ah, yes," she whispered as I ran my thumb over her hardened nipple.

I pulled her up and wrapped my arms around her, picking her up off the counter, her legs wrapped tightly around my waist. Carrying her to her bedroom, I placed her down on the floor. I looked down into those innocent eyes I'd grown to love and again brought my lips to hers. Bringing my fingers to the front of her jeans, I flicked the button open and gently pushed them over her hips, letting them fall to the floor.

She stood there, not moving, hiding her eyes from me. "What is it?" I asked quietly, lifting her chin.

She shook her head, not saying anything.

I didn't want to bring it up, but I had to. I had to know what I was suspecting. "Am I the first, after..."

Her eyes met mine, and she nodded her head. "The only other," she whispered.

I was about to stop, to really make sure this was okay, when I felt her small hands tug at my belt. With heated cheeks, she fumbled a bit, finally undoing it, then flicking the button open.

I brought my lips to hers, kissing her again. I jumped when I felt her small hand run over my hard cock. Her light touch was like torture, until she gripped my cock through my boxers. She pressed her lips to my chest and ran her hand down to cup my balls.

My body was on fire. I grabbed her and backed her up to the bed, gently putting her down and laying her back. I kicked my jeans from my feet and pulled my wallet from my back pocket, quickly pulling out the condom I'd slipped in there earlier. I wanted to take her and make her mine, but tonight wasn't about that. Tonight, had to be about tenderness.

Peggy

I felt his rough fingers at my waist, playing with the band of my panties. I wanted him to take them off. I reached behind me, unsnapping my bra, allowing it to fall away from my skin. I quickly slipped out of it and dropped it onto the floor. I looked up to see him kneeling between my legs.

He leaned over, bent down, and circled each of my nipples with his tongue and gently blew on them. The heat from his tongue mixed with the cool air of his breath was almost my undoing. It was then I felt his fingers trail down my legs, taking my panties with them. Placing his hands on the backs of my thighs, he pushed me open, his eyes falling to my center.

"Hold your legs, baby," he whispered. "I can't wait to taste you."

I almost jumped right off the bed the second his tongue connected with me, and I arched my back as he began lapping and sucking away at my center.

"Oh god," I cried, tilting my head back on the bed. "Stop, you've got to stop."

Ethan didn't listen, not even a little. Instead, it was as if I told him the opposite. Sucking and licking at that sensitive little bud, he only added to it when he slid his finger inside of me, then added another.

"So, fucking tight," he whispered. "So fucking wet, so damn good." His mouth connected with my center again as he pumped his fingers into me, curling until he hit that special spot inside of me.

"Ethan..."

"Hold on, baby. Don't let go just yet," he whispered, placing a kiss on my inner thigh before climbing to his knees. I opened my eyes in time to see him rip open a condom wrapper. I watched as he slid the condom over his hardened cock. "Ready?" he asked, pressing himself into me.

I nodded, waiting to feel him. He slid in slowly, a little at a time, closing his eyes and groaning with every movement he made. His hands interlocked with mine as he slid himself in all the way, breathing hard as he stilled.

"Fuck, you feel...amazing."

"Ethan..." I cried, clenching around him.

Wrapping his arms around me, he began slowly pumping into me, long strokes followed by deep and hard, hitting that spot inside of me with each pump. My fingers dug into his back with every movement he made.

"Ethan, I can't hold back..." I whispered breathlessly.

"Don't...just let yourself go..." he said as I clenched tighter around him. I could feel him swelling inside of me.

I held back as long as I could, finally letting my climax go. Digging my fingers into his back, he began pumping faster and harder, until I felt his muscles tighten and he finally let go, spilling into me.

Ethan

Night had fallen. We'd drifted off to sleep, but now I lay awake. I was ready for more. I was fifty, but I felt like I was twenty again. The second I'd been inside of this woman, I knew she was the one.

She shifted in my arms, bringing her back against my

chest. I kissed the side of her neck, down to her bare shoulder, and brought my left hand up and cupped her breast. When I heard a little moan escape her lips, I lightly pinched her hardening nipple.

Her left hand moved to my hip, where it now rested. "Ethan?"

"Yeah, baby, it's me," I whispered breathlessly as I bit her earlobe.

Holding her, I allowed my left hand to travel down her body to the spot between her legs. She was so relaxed against me. I slid my finger into her slit. She was already wet, so I put just a little pressure on her clit.

"Oh god," she murmured.

"That's right." I rolled her nipple between my thumb and forefinger, listening as she gasped. "You want more?" I questioned, once again running my finger through her slit.

"Yes," she said, bringing her hand against mine, trying to guide it back down between her legs.

"Are you sure?"

"Yes." This time her voice was louder, a little more impatient.

My cock ached as I once again ran my finger over the tiny bundle of nerves, making her squirm in my arms. This time I kept my fingers there, focusing on that little spot that was driving her crazy, and then I moved them away.

"Ethan…" she cried, digging her fingers into my arm. "Stop teasing me."

"I'm not…"

"Yes…you…"

I brought my fingers back to the spot she loved. She let out a loud moan as I worked over her in small circles, bringing her so close to the edge, only to stop again.

"You're killing me, and you're so hard. I want you inside me," she whispered, as she wrapped her hand around my cock.

"Peggy, are you telling me you want my cock?" I whispered in her ear.

I raised myself up onto my forearm. "Tell me what you want," I said, my voice low and thick with need.

I couldn't contain myself anymore. Grabbing her, I rolled her over in my arms, grabbed her leg, and pulled her on top of me. Her face was bathed in the light coming in through the window, and while I fumbled around for the other condom I'd left on the bedside table, I saw her shake her head.

"You're sure?" I questioned.

She didn't answer me. She took my hands with hers and, straddling me, she lined me up at her entrance and worked her way down onto my cock. Her tightness swallowed every inch of me.

"How's that feel, baby?" I gritted, trying to control my release.

"I'm so...so full...so good," she breathed, closing her eyes, interlocking her fingers with mine.

I gripped her hips as she rested her hands on my chest and started moving her hips. I could already feel my orgasm building, threatening to rip through me. There was no controlling it. The closer I got, the closer she got, and the faster she moved, and soon her head had dropped back and she was screaming my name again.

Peggy

I sat in the kitchen sipping coffee, while Ethan was in the shower. I flipped the pages of the magazine I was reading, thinking about last night. Ethan hadn't left after the third time. Instead, he'd slipped from the bed and had surprised me by returning with a hot cloth. He cleaned me up and then slid in beside me, pulling me into his arms.

We talked for a bit and lay together. Then, in the comfort of his arms, I slipped into a much-needed deep sleep. When I awoke this morning, I was still expecting him to be gone. I don't know why, but I figured he'd run. Instead, I opened my eyes and found him spooned against me, his arm wrapped securely around my waist. I'd tried to slip from his embrace, but when I moved, he only tightened his grasp on me, pulling me back and placing a kiss on my bare shoulder.

We'd shared a coffee this morning in the comfort of my bed before getting up. I showered first, and then he jumped in. Things seemed to feel different between us this morning—not in a bad way, just different.

I took another sip of coffee and flipped the page of my magazine, returning to the article I'd been reading when Ethan stepped from the bedroom.

He came over to me and placed a kiss on my lips, then poured himself a cup of coffee and sat down across from me. "So, what is on your schedule for today?" he asked.

"Well, I have some arrangements to make at the shop. Then Trinity and I are going to visit Brooke, and then out to the retirement home to visit Vi and Jed. We're delivering that lovely gift basket that Vi won at the festival from the pottery store. What about you?"

He looked around the kitchen and living room, a slight frown on his face. "Well, I'm not sure if you noticed, but you have a crack in the tile of your shower floor."

"I know. I saw that a couple of weeks ago." I shrugged.

Ethan looked at me. "Have you called in anyone to repair it?"

I shook my head. I knew this place needed a lot of work. I also hated being reminded of the fact, since I had such little time to get it done. "I know I should. It's just I work six days a week, and no maintenance worker in Willow Valley will work on a Sunday. I've been doing the best I can."

"I know. I just wanted to tell you because I'd hate to see you have to deal with a lot of water damage. I could patch it up for you today if you like."

Something inside of me made me shake my head. "No, you've done enough helping me with all the other messes around here. I'll get it done," I said, looking at the mug that sat in my hands.

Whatever the reason, I wondered if he was taking pity on me. After all, I was a widow who had told him enough sob stories to make him feel he needed to stick around. The last thing I wanted was for him to feel he had to do these things for me out of pity.

"Peggy, you know, I've been thinking a lot about this. About us. This place is a lot to keep up with. I'm wondering if you've ever given any thought to moving?" Ethan asked.

I shook my head and frowned. "No. Besides, where would I move to?"

A smile came to Ethan's lips. "Well, I was thinking, you helped me pick out that gorgeous property, and it's big for a single guy. I'd love to share it with you. Why don't you give some thought to moving in with me?"

"Ethan..." I paused, my stomach flipping at the thought of accepting the fact that I was more than ready to move on from just about everything in my life aside from my shop. "Honestly, I'm doing the best I can," I said, swallowing hard.

"I know. But, sweetie, I've watched you struggle for a few months now. It can be easier," he said, placing his large hand on mine. "We can tackle things together, as a couple."

I shook my head as I fought back tears. I wasn't supposed be feeling like this. I shouldn't have all this panic, all this anxiety about taking another step forward when last night we took probably the biggest step we'd ever taken together. It was supposed to get easier. Wasn't it?

"I was thinking we could get this place ready to sell, while getting the new place ready to move into. Then we'll put this one up for sale or we could keep it as a rental. Then perhaps, once we are settled, we could take a vacation together. After we return, we can have Trinity, Thomas, Brooke, and Tristan over for dinner in our new home. Once we are settled, of course."

I sat there, my arms crossed in front of me, irritated. "I see you have everything planned out. I'm sorry, Ethan. I'm just not ready." A tear slipped down my cheek before I had a chance to wipe it away.

The room grew silent. I could feel him watching me as I sat there trying to find the words to explain how I felt, but nothing came. Finally, Ethan cleared his throat and got up from his chair. I watched as he took his coat from the hook beside the door and grabbed the handle of the door. I wanted to tell him not to go, but somehow, I was frozen to the spot in which I sat. He stood there for a moment, facing the door, his shoulders rising and falling at a rapid pace.

"I'm sorry you feel this way. I really thought you were ready to move forward with me, with us."

"Ethan..."

"When you are ready...if I am free, and still around here, I'll gladly revisit things, but right now, my heart can't take any more of this up and down. I was certain you were ready for things last night, but it appears that I was wrong."

I stood up, panic filling me at the thought of losing him. I was about to step forward, to tell him I wanted to talk and work things out, when he held his hand out, stopping me in my tracks.

"I mean it, Peggy, I can't take it. One minute you're fine with us and the next, well, it ends like this. You not being ready. I wanted something with you, something meaningful. I'm not a kid. I mean what I say and do. I thought you knew that. There are no games with me. I commit, I commit wholeheartedly. I understand you went through something horrible, but it's been eight years. It's time for you to move on."

I stared at Ethan through blurry eyes. The hurt on his face was more than I could bear seeing. The hurt in my heart was one I could barely stand feeling. The longer he stood there, the longer it felt as if there was a hot knife searing through my chest.

As Ethan went to grab the handle, anger erupted from inside of me. "No, Ethan...don't tell me how I should feel. It's not time I move on. See, you don't understand, so please stop saying you do." I clenched and unclenched my fists at my sides. "He was taken from me when I was angry. I'd said so many things I didn't mean, and I will never get the chance to undo the words. Do you have any idea how that feels? Not to be forgiven for the things you said when you were angry."

"We all say things when we are angry."

"Yep, and all I do is keep wondering what part of the words I'd said to him went through his head as the oncoming car smashed into his. What he really thought of me as he lay on the pavement dying. So don't stand there and tell me you know how I feel because you don't. Polly got sick. You had time to say good-bye to her before she was gone."

"Peggy..."

I turned my back on him. I didn't want to hear anything he had to say. I wanted him gone from my sight.

"Get out." They were the only words I could manage. Any more than that, I'd be a heap of tears.

Ethan was quiet for a moment, and then he cleared his throat, and for the first time since I'd known the man, he raised his voice.

"Peggy, you only know what I've chosen to tell you about Polly. You know she got sick, but there are things you don't know. You don't know that I was on a mission when she found out. That she went through the diagnosis alone, the treatment alone because I refused to believe that there was something wrong with her. She was also alone when she learned that the treatment had stopped working and was given the news that she only had another one to two weeks to live. When she told me the news, I still refused to believe it.

"When I finally came to terms with it, I was stuck in some shithole airport over in some war-torn country, while my wife lay in a hospital bed in pain, dying, when I should have been with her. To hold her and comfort her. It was more important for me not to deal with how I felt and to be on a mission than to be with my family. Instead, because I didn't want to face the truth, my wife died alone instead of with me by her side. The guilt I felt over that almost fucking killed me. It took me years to let it go. So, believe me when I say I fucking get it."

I fought back the tears as he looked at me and shook his head. I didn't know what had really happened with his wife's sickness. Through all his letters, he had made it sound as if he'd been there for her when, in reality, he hadn't, and because of that, he too blamed himself.

"This may sound cruel as fuck, so I'll apologize now. I spent the better part of the last fifteen years living in hell because I couldn't forgive myself for not being able to accept the truth. I lost all those years, but you have a chance to not do the same thing I did. It's time you realize you aren't the one who died in that accident. Just like I had to learn to forgive myself for not being able to accept the fact I lost my wife."

He pulled the door open and took off down the stairs to his truck while I stood there. When I heard the engine start and saw him pull out of the driveway, I ran over and slammed the door shut. I was angry because everything he'd said had been true. He wasn't playing; I knew that. I also knew I had been treating myself as if I'd been dead for years. I'd allowed the guilt from that night to consume me. I'd held onto it to punish myself, and I was using it once again to avoid the possibility of a new relationship with a wonderful man. The problem was, I'd held it for so that I didn't know how to let it go.

"You are really quiet today. Everything okay?" Trinity asked for the third time as we drove out to the retirement home to visit Vi.

I'd contemplated not going. I'd spent half the morning picking up the phone, dialing Trinity's number, then hanging up before it rang. I'd even called in and told the girls I wouldn't be in the store. The last thing I felt like doing was going to visit Vi and Jed and being upbeat.

"It's nothing," I mumbled.

"Peggy, you haven't said a word since you got in the car. You didn't even congratulate me on selling almost all those old books I found in that sale I had."

"When did you do that?" I questioned, completely distraught.

"I just told you. The sale ended yesterday."

"Oh," I mumbled as I looked out the window as we drove down the country road. "I must have forgotten."

"Peggy, what is going on?"

I was so focused on my own thoughts, I didn't hear Trinity ask that question. In fact, I didn't hear her the second or third time she asked me either. Finally, I noticed when she slammed on the brakes and sent me flying against my seatbelt.

"What are you doing?" I yelled, completely startled at the fact that nothing was in front of the car to make her stop like that.

"I'm getting your attention. Now, before we go any further, tell me what is going on?"

I looked over at my friend, and that was when the tears began pouring down my cheeks. Instantly, Trinity pulled the car over to the side of the road and, once the car was safely in park, she leaned over and pulled me in for a hug.

"What happened?" she asked.

"I don't know how we got to this point," I cried.

"What point? Who?"

"Ethan and I. He spent the night last night and we... and this morning he..." I sobbed, not making any sense.

"You what? He what?" Trinity questioned.

"We slept together...and this morning he asked me to move in with him. I'm not ready, Trinity. I can't." I looked at my friend through tear-filled eyes.

"What? You slept together...as in..."

I met her eyes and nodded. "It was so wonderful," I sniffled. "Unlike anything I've ever had."

"I knew you two were getting serious." She said in a low voice, her thumb tapping on the steering wheel.

"We did, we were...and then he asked me to move in."

"And?"

"When I told him I wasn't ready, he ended things. Told me when I was ready, really ready, to come to him, and if he were free, he'd consider talking things through. He told me his heart couldn't take these games."

"What games Peggy?" Trinity questioned, more lost than I was in this moment.

Half an hour later, Trinity and I sat on the hood of her car as she listened while I told her all the other things he'd said—about his wife and how he handled it. Then I told her the part about me not being the one who died. She said nothing. She simply listened, nodding her head until I finished. That was when she let out a loud sigh and looked at me.

"Goodness, I don't even know where to start, so I'll start at the start. What is it you're having such a hard time with?" she asked.

I sat there quietly for a few moments, thinking about my answer. Truth was, I felt as if I were losing Darren all over again, only this time, it was me leaving him. I knew he was never coming back. Yet somehow, I felt that perhaps holding onto him, to his memory, may make him return to me one day.

"Peggy, Darren isn't coming back," Trinity said, her voice low.

"I know," I replied, my voice shaking.

"I hate to admit it, but Ethan is right. You aren't the one who died. You need to stop punishing yourself."

Trinity had hit it on the head. Darren wasn't coming back, and all I'd been doing these past years was exactly that. Punishing myself because I was the one who ran away from him after the fight we'd had, for never getting to apologize to him for being angry at him. I'd been doing this to myself for never getting to tell him I loved him again, even though he knew how I felt.

The instant her words sunk in, the floodgates opened, and the tears poured out. We sat on the edge of the country road, while I cried until there were no more tears to cry. When I looked over at my friend, she looked at me with concern lining her face.

"You, okay?" she asked.

I wiped away the few remaining tears and nodded. "I am."

"Good, now, I don't think we should go out to visit Vi and Jed. We will reschedule for another afternoon. It's almost dinnertime. I think we should head back to town. I'm going to take you home, you're going to have a hot bath, and as much as you probably don't want to, I think you need to call Ethan and talk."

Ethan

Two weeks later

It was after seven by the time I finally sat down for the first time in my new home. The mess of boxes and furniture that lay around only told me how much work I still had ahead of me to finish, but for tonight, my work was done.

I rested my head back against my new recliner and closed my eyes for a moment. It had been a long day, and even though I still had to put my bed together before I could sleep, I needed to take a minute and pause.

Melinda had been a big help. She and Cici had arrived early this morning and began unpacking all the kitchen dishes. While they did that, I directed the furniture delivery crew where to place things. Then the girls had gone down to The Crispy Biscuit and picked up dinner, bringing it back for the three of us to share. It was nice having the first dinner at my place with my daughter and her friend. However, the only thing that would have made it better was if Peggy could have been here.

I sat in the silence of my living room, the memory of the words I'd said to her running through my mind once again, just as they'd been doing ever since they'd fallen from my lips. I'd thought about her for days. I'd even driven past her store numerous times, trying to build up the nerve to go and apologize.

The first time I'd driven by, I'd seen her inside alone. I'd pulled up to the curb across the street and had climbed out of my truck in time to see a customer step inside the store. This wasn't something I wanted anyone else to hear, so I got in the truck and drove away.

The second time I'd seen her, she'd been in her garden at home, weeding away. I was about to talk to her when one of the girls from the shop stepped out of her small shed. She said something to Peggy. They both laughed, and then she sat down beside her to help with the weeding.

I'd given up for a few days, and then there was yesterday. I'd come back in from Cedar Landing and was about to stop in when I noticed Trinity's car parked out front. So, I'd left. Which brought me to now. I didn't have the internet hooked up yet, so even if my computer was unpacked, I couldn't even send her an email to let her know I was thinking of her.

I blew out a breath and got up from my chair and made my way over to the phone I'd had installed last night. I dialed her number. On the fourth ring, I grew worried. Peggy, no matter how angry, always answered the phone, that much I knew. Instead, I tried the shop. That line, too, did nothing but ring.

I glanced at my watch. The shop would still be open, I thought to myself. I grabbed my keys from the table and hopped into my truck. It only took me a few minutes to navigate through the streets and come to the front of Peggy's Petals. I could see a note taped to the front door but couldn't read it, so I hopped out of the truck and ran up.

"Closed. Had to go to Cedar Landing for supplies. Re-opens tomorrow at seven. Sorry for the inconvenience."

Peggy

I wrapped the black sweater I wore tightly around me. It was a cool evening, too cold to be sitting beside the water.

I dug my little shovel into the dirt and plopped the little purple petunia into the hole, filling it back in.

"I didn't just come all this way to plant these flowers. I came to talk to you about something important," I whispered to the headstone. I acted as if all the other headstones could hear me as well.

I popped another petunia out of the pack and slipped it into the ground. "You always liked these flowers, said they were too friendly." I smiled. "You were right. They are disgustingly happy, but they didn't sell well this year, and I didn't want them to go to waste."

I emptied the pack of flowers and placed the empty tray into the basket I'd brought. "I can sense you are impatient. You want to know why I'm here. I need you to know something."

I looked over my shoulder at the sound of a car door slamming shut and saw a young girl and her mother carrying a small basket of flowers. I smiled to myself as I watched them make their way over to a grave where the young girl placed the basket of flowers down, smiling sadly at her mother. Then they both bowed their heads.

"I'm sorry for what happened the night of your accident. I'm sorry I got so angry at you. It wasn't fair to you, the way I acted, especially after you gave me such a wonderful gift." I swallowed hard as I looked out over the water. "I hope you can forgive me."

I paused, taking a moment to just look at the scenery in front of me as I formed the words in my mind.

"I met someone, Darren. Someone I like very much. In fact, I think I'm in love with him. It's taken me days to figure that out and to be somewhat okay with it. As much as I don't want to tell you this part, I need to say it. We took an important step a few nights ago, and now he's asked me to move in with him," I said, swallowing hard.

I sat there, hearing another car door shut, and turned to see the girl and her mother get into their car and pull away from the curb. Glancing around the cemetery, I was once again the only one here. I let out a breath and turned back to look at Darren's headstone, my eyes blurring with tears.

"I'm having a hard time with things, Darren. I can't forgive myself. I can't move past you and let you go because if I hadn't flipped out, you never would have left me. You'd have been right behind me and home with me for dinner."

I buried my face in my hands and cried. "I need to forgive myself or I need you to forgive me. Let me know you know I loved you. I just wish you could give me some sort of sign." I wiped the tears from my cheeks.

A large splash in the water caused me to look up in time to see the same lone Trumpeter swan swimming once again in the water. It began swimming toward me, staring right at me, before he turned and swam in another direction just as thunder roared above me. I felt a drop of rain, and then a streak of lightning bolted through the sky. I watched as the swan lifted its body out of the water and took off in flight, just as another crack of thunder roared above.

I looked up at the darkening sky and gathered my things. Feeling a couple of drops of rain as I made my way to the car, I climbed in just in time for the skies to open and rain to pour down.

Sitting there for a few minutes, until the downpour let up a bit, I then started the car and pulled away.

I stopped into the local coffee shop and grabbed a coffee and muffin before starting back to Willow Valley. It was darker than it should have been with the storm. That, combined with the heavy rain and lack of streetlights, was making it hard to see once I was outside of Cedar Landing city limits. I glanced at the clock on my dash; it was just about 8, so I flipped the radio on to catch one of my favourite programs.

It only took one second for my eyes to leave the road. One second to see a flash of light, and something or someone standing in the road, right in the path of my vehicle, and I swerved. That was the last thing I remembered.

Ethan

I stood in my living room, pacing back and forth, as I watched the storm out the window. I glanced at my watch. It was 9. Walking over to the phone, I dialed Peggy's number again. I'd been calling every fifteen minutes, but like all the times before, all it did was ring. She should have been back by now, I thought to myself.

Pacing once again, I decided to call Bluebird Books. On the second ring, Trinity answered the phone. "Hello, Bluebird Books."

"Trinity, it's Ethan."

"Hey, Ethan. You're lucky you caught me. I was just getting ready to head up to the apartment for the night. What can I do for you?"

"You haven't heard from Peggy by chance?" I asked, swallowing hard.

"No, I'm sorry, I haven't. I know she was heading out to Cedar Landing today, but I am sure she is back by now."

"I've tried calling. She hasn't answered."

"Did you try the store?"

"I did. No answer there either."

"Well, perhaps her phone is down. Sometimes that happens in these storms here. I wouldn't worry about it. I know she doesn't answer the shop phone once the place is closed, though. So perhaps that is why you can't get her."

"Okay." The nagging feeling in the pit of my stomach still told me this wasn't right.

"Maybe try her again. She also could be out at the grocery store as well. It is her grocery night," Trinity said, trying to be reassuring.

"Okay," I said, still feeling uneasy. "I'm sorry to bother you."

"Never a bother. Have a good night, Ethan."

"You too."

I hung up the phone and looked out the window, the rain falling harder now than before. The nagging feeling in the pit of my stomach was getting worse, and I knew it wouldn't calm down until I knew she was okay. I grabbed my keys and headed to my truck.

I drove up Cardinal Street to Peggy's house. The lights were off, and there was no car in the driveway. My stomach began turning, so I continued over to the flower shop, only to see the same thing. Lights off, no car, and the note still hung up in the window. I looked up the road and then in my rearview mirror. The street was empty.

Instead of going back home, I took off toward Cedar Landing. It was hard to see out in the dark, but I took my time. Finally, the rain sort of slowed, making the drive a little easier. I was just about to Cedar Landing when a flash of light caught my eye over to the right side. I slowed down and backed up. I got out of my truck and looked down into the ditch and there, deep in the ditch, was Peggy's car. I looked over the edge of the road to see the front end of her car submerged in the water that had accumulated from the rain. It was too dark to see, so I ran back and grabbed the flashlight out of the back of my truck.

Rain pelting down, I carefully climbed down the slippery embankment to where I could look inside her car. I turned on the flashlight and shone it on the window. Immediately, I saw her laying against the steering wheel. Panic filled me. I tried to open the door, but it was locked. "Fuck."

I banged on the window, hoping to wake her, but it did no good. I looked around and then thought for a moment before I ran back to my truck grabbing the toolbox from behind my seat, I pulled out a hammer and went back over to the car. Taking the claw of the hammer, I placed it up against the edge of the window and hit it, watching the glass shatter.

Getting my hand inside, I unlocked the door and pulled it open. I unhooked her seatbelt and then carefully got hold of her. She was out cold, blood covering her face from a gash on her forehead.

"Peggy. Peggy," I said as I shook her, but she didn't respond. I felt for a pulse, and once I felt a faint one, I carefully pulled her from the car, throwing her up and over my shoulder. I took her over to my truck, where I laid her in the front seat, then I ran around to the driver's side, hopped in, and took off toward Cedar Landing to the hospital I'd remembered passing.

Peggy

I blinked a few times, my vision blurry. The sound of steady beeping drilling into my brain, driving me crazy. I looked around at the unfamiliar surroundings. I looked to my side to see a monitor of some sort and looked down at my hand to see a clip on my finger. Then I noticed an enormous bunch of red roses placed on a table beside me. I frowned. *Where was I? A hospital? Why was I in the hospital?*

"Hello," I called, hoping I wasn't alone in the room, since someone had pulled curtains around both sides of my bed.

"One moment," a voice answered.

I waited for a few moments, when finally, a woman poked her head around the curtain. "You're awake. I will have to get the doctor," she said, scurrying away before I could ask her questions.

"Mrs. Hollis." A doctor stepped up beside my bed. "How are you feeling?"

"Um, my head hurts a little. What happened? Where am I?" I asked.

"You are at Cedar Landing General. Three days ago, you arrived in our emergency department. Your car spun out in the rainstorm we had. You hit your head."

I thought for a moment, remembering driving home in that horrible rain. "Yes, there was a flash of lightning, and I saw someone or something in the middle of the road," I said, nodding.

"Well, whatever the cause, you hit your head badly and were unconscious when you were brought in here," the doctor said, looking into my eyes.

"Who brought me here?" I questioned.

The doctor wrote something in the file he held and then flipped back a few pages. "A friend of yours, Ethan Alexander," he replied.

"Ethan?" I questioned. That wasn't possible. Ethan hadn't known I was coming to Cedar Landing. In fact, I hadn't spoken to him since the day he walked out of my kitchen.

"Yes. He brought you in. Apparently, he found your car after it had slid off the road," he said, reading something on my chart.

It was then that I heard a familiar female voice. Trinity came rushing into the room, followed by Thomas. "Oh my god, you're finally awake!" she cried, rushing over to me.

I smiled at my best friend. "Yes. Hi, Thomas."

"You gave us a good scare," Thomas said, patting my leg.

"What happened?" Trinity asked.

"Whoa, everyone, please, calm down," the doctor said. "I want to examine this cut and give Peggy a once-over now that she's awake," he said, his voice quieter. He pressed around on my forehead, causing me to flinch.

I looked over at Trinity, trying to ignore that the doctor was causing me a little pain. "Is Ethan here? Can I see him?" I questioned.

"I'm afraid not. He isn't here," Trinity answered. "He brought you in, stayed a while, left the flowers, and called us. He hasn't been here since."

I closed my eyes as the doctor continued his examination, trying not to flinch as he pressed around, my head beginning to pound.

"The stitches look good and clean. How does your head feel? Any dizziness?"

"Aside from a little headache now, I feel okay. No dizziness right now," I said.

"Good. Well, we will get you a little dinner. We'd like to keep you a couple more nights, and as long as you're feeling okay, you should be able to head home the day after tomorrow. Of course, you will need someone to pick you up."

I nodded. "Sounds good."

"I'll pick her up," Trinity offered immediately.

"Perfect," the doctor said, then asked to see the nurse outside, leaving me with Thomas and Trinity to find out exactly what had happened.

Two days passed rather quickly. I'd had no symptoms of a concussion, just a dull headache, which the doctor was sure would pass with time. He gave me some medication and discharged me into Trinity's care. I now sat in the front seat of Trinity's car, holding the vase full of red roses on my lap. Trinity carefully pulled out of the parking lot, heading toward Willow Valley.

"I'm so glad you are okay. I was so upset and worried when Ethan called and told us. I almost dragged Thomas out of bed to drive me out to the hospital, even though there was nothing we could have done."

I looked at my best friend. "How did he even find me?" I asked.

"Funny thing, he called me the night you had gone

out there. Apparently, he had tried to come and see you but returned home when he found out you'd gone. Yet around nine he called me at the store and asked me if I'd heard from you. I didn't give his worry any thought. I knew you were upset with him. I figured perhaps you just needed some time."

I nodded. "And?"

"Well, I guess he went to see if you were home after we had gotten off the phone and you weren't. He then went to the shop. I guess the worry got the best of him, so he just drove off toward Cedar Landing. That's when he found you, just about ten minutes outside of Cedar Landing."

"You mean he drove all that way in that storm?"

Trinity nodded. "He did. He told me he had a feeling you were in some sort of trouble."

"He left me these too," I said, looking at the flowers.

"He did." She smiled. "He was at the hospital the next morning when I arrived. He was a mess. He's been over at our place for the past three days, working with Thomas in the shop to keep himself busy."

I frowned. "What about his new place?" I asked, looking at my best friend. "He just moved in. Shouldn't he be unpacking?"

She smiled. "Well, I asked him the same thing. He told me it could wait. That it didn't really mean much now. You were all that mattered."

Tears clouded my eyes. "But...he said all those things to me."

"I know he did. He knows it too. He's been talking to Thomas a lot."

I sat there thinking about what Trinity had just said. "Trinity, I feel that I've messed up."

"It's okay, you're allowed to mess up. Love isn't supposed to be perfect. It's supposed to be messy. I think, when you are ready, that you two need to talk and figure things out, but, Peggy, just know the man is a mess."

As Trinity drove toward Willow Valley, I rested my head back against the seat and looked down at the roses I held on my lap. Red roses, everyone knew, meant love. Did that mean that Ethan really did love me? I let out a breath. I couldn't wait to get back home.

Ethan

I stood just outside of Peggy's home, Thomas standing beside me. We'd just picked up a load of lumber from the hardware store and I'd asked that he drop me at Peggy's. She'd been home for a few days now, and I couldn't wait any longer to see her.

"Did you want me to wait?" he asked, as we both stood looking over at her small house.

"No. If she kicks me to the curb, I'll just come and get my truck and know that it's over." I shrugged.

"Don't be ridiculous, you can call me. I'll come back." He joked, "I'm not the one mad at you. Go get her."

"Thanks. See you later."

"Just call the shop if you need a lift!" Thomas yelled out as I crossed the street. I turned and waved to my friend and prayed I didn't need to call him to come and get me.

I walked over to the door, brought my hand up, and knocked. Then I stood back, waiting for Peggy to answer. It had been a few minutes, and I was about to knock again when the door slowly opened, and Peggy peeked out. She said nothing. She just softly smiled and opened the door a little farther, enough for me to step inside.

"How are you feeling?" I questioned.

"I'm okay," she said, closing the door. "Small headache, but I've been taking the medication the doctor prescribed."

I looked around her small living room, noticing the roses I'd gotten for her sitting on the side table. I went to turn back to her, to apologize for what I'd said to her the morning after we'd slept together, when she surprised me by wrapping her arms around me.

"Thank you," she mumbled into my chest. "Thank you for trusting me enough to share what happened between you and Polly, and thank you for still caring enough to come out and find me."

I slowly wrapped my arms around her, pulling her small frame against me. "I was so worried. I knew almost instantly something was wrong. All I could think about was finding you, making sure you were all right."

"How did you find me?"

I walked her over to the couch and together we sat down. "Honestly, I don't know. I just had a bad feeling, so I came to see if you were home. You weren't here, you weren't at the shop, so I figured I'd just take a drive, in case you broke down somewhere. It was dark, the rain was just coming down, making it hard to see. I don't know how I even saw your car. It was so far down into the ditch, it wasn't possible to see it from the road. All I remember was seeing a flash of light, and I thought that, perhaps, your bumper caught the headlight of my truck," I said, thinking back to that night, still unsure how the hell it happened. "Once I saw your car, I knew it wasn't the light from the bumper because it wasn't even visible from the road."

"The ditches are so deep out there."

I nodded. "I know. I'm still not sure how I found you, to be honest. When I finally left the hospital, I had a hard time finding the car for the tow truck, and that was in the daylight, with no rain."

"Do you know where my car is?"

"I had it towed to my place. There's a lot of damage to the front end, and I'm not sure insurance will repair it. I had someone from the garage out to look at it. He wasn't very hopeful."

Peggy nodded, then looked at me. "Thank you. Thank you for coming out there."

"No problem. I'm just glad I found you. I don't know what might have happened had I not of."

We sat in silence for a few moments, then she scooted over toward me and curled herself into my side, resting her head on my shoulder. "It doesn't matter," she responded.

"Yes, it does." My voice shook. My normal confidence was gone, because for the first time I was about to admit, with words, my feelings for her. I had to. I needed her to know how I felt, even if it wasn't going to be returned. "Peggy, I was afraid that something was going to happen to you before I could actually tell you how I felt about you."

Peggy looked up at me and placed her hand on my chest, fiddling with the button on my shirt until it opened. She traced over one letter of my tattoo and met my eyes. "You already did."

I frowned. "No, I didn't."

She softly smiled. "You did. The red roses. I got the message through the meaning of the flowers." Her eyes filled with tears. "It was a wonderful message to wake up to."

My hand cupped her cheek, and I brushed away her tears with my thumb before I took her mouth with mine, kissing her hard. She was right. I'd forgotten about the meaning behind the flowers. I didn't speak the language of flowers. Hell, I could barely speak the language of love with actual words. As our lips parted, her blue eyes met mine. "I'm almost afraid to say it..." she whispered, her voice shaking as well.

"You don't need to say anything," I said, pulling her in close. "Say it when you're ready."

Peggy rested her hand on my cheek. "I need to say it too because...I love you, too. I want you to know that. I'm sorry it's taken me so long to realize it."

"Whoa, Peggy, don't—" I didn't want her to say it because she felt she had to.

She stopped me by placing her finger in front of my lips. "No, Ethan, it's the truth. I know how you found me."

I frowned. "How hard did you hit your head?" I joked.

"Just listen to me. The night of the storm, I stopped in at the cemetery before coming back home. I went to Darren's grave so I could talk to him. You know I've been having a hard time because I've been blaming myself for his death. I've been blaming myself for many things, and it needed to stop."

"I know...but you shouldn't blame yourself. You need to let it go. Allow yourself to heal."

"I have been. This was the last step I needed to take to let it all go. See, I said a lot of things to Darren that night, things I never meant, and after I said them, I rushed away in a hurry. I was angry. Only, I never got the chance to apologize, and I never got to tell him one more time how much I loved him."

"You've been torturing yourself."

"I have. But when I went there, I talked to him. You may think that's stupid, but I asked him that night to give me a sign, a sign that told me he knew I loved him. I also told him about you. That I'd met you and that I thought I was falling in love with you. Maybe that is how you found me? Maybe he made it possible."

I looked at Peggy, at the light in her eyes, at the possibility that perhaps she'd gotten the answer she'd needed. "Maybe it was him," I replied.

She rested her head on my shoulder. "I want to stay," she said, her voice low.

Unsure of what she meant by stay, I said nothing. I wrapped my arms around her and pulled her against me, holding her.

"Did you hear me?"

"Yes, you want to stay."

She looked up at me. "Yes, I want to stay with you. If you'll still have me?"

I placed my finger under her chin and tilted her head back, slowly bringing my mouth to hers. Kissing her gently at first, my tongue parted her lips and swept through her mouth. The longer we kissed, the more frantic it became, and soon we parted, breathless. "I'll have you." I winked. "I can't wait, but only when you're ready. So, however long it takes. I'll be here, waiting. I'm not going anywhere."

Peggy

I shoved the picnic basket into the back of the truck, followed by the small picnic blanket I'd brought. Ethan closed the small hibachi we'd brought with us and carried it over to the back of the truck, sliding it in, then closing up the tailgate.

"Lunch was amazing. A suitable reward after a hard morning of car shopping," he said, pulling me in for a kiss. "I don't think I'll ever tire of your kebabs." He brought both his hands up to my breasts, cupping them in his hands.

"Oh my god. Ethan!" I squealed, pushing his hands away. "We're in the middle of a park, with kids around," I whispered.

"I meant your shish kebabs. You dirty girl," he said, kissing my neck again, embracing me. "So, what if someone sees us? They'll just think we are in love, which we are."

I allowed myself to relax against his body as he claimed my mouth.

"Thanks for helping me get that car," I said, smiling at him as I slipped from his embrace. "I love it. Best part, there will be more than enough room to deliver flowers from it. Plus, you got me an excellent deal. So, how could I not reward you with your favourite meal?"

Ethan chuckled. "I can think of one other meal I prefer, and perhaps I'll help myself to that tonight," he said, gripping my ass as he kissed his way down my neck to my shoulder.

"You're so bad," I said, my cheeks heating at his suggestion.

"Yeah, that may be, but last I recall, you love it. Plus, you're just as bad."

We'd driven out the Cedar Landing to find a new car for me. The other couldn't be repaired after the accident. Too much damage had been done. I had no choice but to get something new. "You ready to make our way back?"

"Yeah, but I was wondering, could we stop somewhere on our way?"

"Of course," Ethan said, helping me get into the front of the truck. "Where to?" he asked, hopping into the driver's seat.

I gave him directions as we drove, and soon we'd

pulled up alongside the river at the small cemetery in Cedar Landing.

"I hope this is okay, but I wanted you to meet Darren," I said quietly, opening the passenger-side door. When Ethan didn't move, I looked over at him. "This is important to me."

Ethan met my eyes and then cut the engine of his truck and climbed out. I hoped this wouldn't make him too uncomfortable. I was uncomfortable enough for the pair of us. He came around the front of the truck and took my hand in his.

"You okay with this?" I questioned, looking into his eyes.

"Of course," he said, wrapping his arm around me as we made our way over to Darren's grave.

Once there, I knelt on the ground, cleaning up the tiny flower bed I'd made. Once it was back to my standards, I stood up and went over beside Ethan, who wrapped his arm around me in a protective embrace.

"You chose a pleasant spot for him," he said, looking out over the water.

"Yeah, he loved to be on the water, fishing, swimming, boating. I figured it was the best spot." I softly smiled. "Something you both have in common."

"I couldn't agree more," he said, pulling me against him.

We grew quiet as we stood there. I turned to him,

placing my cheek against his chest. "Do you think you could give me a few minutes?" I questioned. "I want to say good-bye."

"Of course, I can, but, baby, you don't need to say good-bye. He's a part of your life…"

"I do," I said. "A part of me just needs to say it."

Ethan held me, squeezing me tighter, and when I looked up at him, he leaned in for a kiss. He then made his way over to the truck. Leaning up against the front of it, he stood there, looking out over the water, giving me the privacy I asked for. I let out a breath and knelt, once again, in front of Darren's grave.

"Darren, I'd like you to meet Ethan," I said quietly, picking the dead flower petals I'd somehow missed from the plants. "He's the one I told you about. He's the man who's looking after me now, and you need to know that he is a good one."

I blinked away the tears that were forming in my eyes and looked up just in time to see the lone Trumpeter swan land on the water. I watched as he swam toward me, when suddenly, from the far side of the river, another swan began swimming toward him.

I smiled as the one that I'd seen before made its way to the bank, climbing up onto the grass. I watched as he began walking toward me just as he had before, then he stopped and stared. I smiled as the other swan joined him.

They both came a little closer, pecked at the ground, and then stopped, looking back over at me.

"Did you finally find your mate?" I asked quietly.

The second swan turned, making its way back to the water, and called out, just as I'd asked my question. The other swan took off toward the water, swimming over to the other one. They both sat there for a moment and then took off down the river together.

I quickly finished clearing up the dead flowers, then stood up and brushed off my pants. "Was that swan my sign?" I questioned, looking down at Darren's name. "It was, wasn't it?" I softly smiled and whispered good-bye to Darren before walking over to where Ethan stood. The minute he noticed me, he opened his arms so I could walk into them.

"You, okay?" he asked, his voice barely above a whisper as he pressed a kiss to my forehead.

"Yes." I rested my head against his chest, taking comfort in his embrace.

"Did you see those swans? I was afraid the one was going to attack you." He chuckled. "They are damn big birds."

I shook my head. "I wasn't. The one is always here. I think he was just coming to tell me he'd found a new mate." I smiled.

Ethan looked at me funny. "What do you mean?"

"Oh, it's a story for another time. We should get

going. Remember, we have dinner plans with Trinity, Thomas, Tristan, and Brooke," I said as I glanced at my watch, noticing the time.

Ethan nodded, pulling me closer against him, and met my lips. "Let's get going."

I kissed him again, then we both climbed into the truck. I watched out the window as Ethan pulled away, and just before we started driving off, the two Trumpeter swans rose out of the water and flew off.

Two Weeks Later

The sliding door off our bedroom opened and Ethan stepped out onto the back deck, carrying two mugs full of coffee.

"Here we go," he said, placing the mugs down on the small glass table before sitting down across from me.

"Beautiful morning, isn't it?" I said, looking out over the lake. The sun was just beginning to rise. We'd started sitting out back in the early mornings on Tuesday. Peggy's Petals was closed for the day, and it gave us the opportunity to spend some private time together. When Ethan said nothing, I turned and looked at him. He sat there, a soft smile on his lips as he watched me.

"Every morning with you is beautiful," he replied, his voice low. "Probably my favorite part of every day is looking at you." He took my hand in his and brought it up to his lips, where he placed a very gentle kiss on the back of my hand. "Are you meeting Trinity this morning?"

"Yes, our usual breakfast date. I thought afterwards we'd head over to the house and start work on painting."

We'd kept my place, planned on fixing it up and using it as a rental property. We had a lot of work ahead of us, but together we knew we could get it done.

"Sounds good. I promised Thomas I'd come by and help him with a delivery this morning. That should give you girls time for breakfast before we get to work on the house."

"Sounds good."

Ethan kicked his feet up and placed them beside mine on the small ottoman, picked up his coffee, and took a sip. Sitting back, he placed his hand over mine. I knew without a doubt that here with him was the place I wanted to be.

I pulled open the door and walked into The Crispy Biscuit. Trinity sat in our usual booth, her nose in a book. I smiled as I walked over to her. It must have been a good one because she didn't lift her eyes from the page, even when the little chimes went off.

"Well, look who's reading a book. Shocker." I smiled.

Trinity looked up at me and shook her head. "What's even more of a shocker is that I'm reading yet another one of these damn political thrillers. Thomas was telling me about this one. He wouldn't shut up about it, and my curiosity got to me."

"Are you keeping secrets from your man?" I asked, sitting down across from her, picking up the book she was reading and giving it a once-over.

"No, I just don't want to let him know he can tell me a plot line and I'll pick up the book. I'll never get to read another romance otherwise."

"That's why I have Ethan talk to Thomas about books. I prefer my romances."

"So, how are things going?" Trinity questioned, sipping her coffee. "You finally all settled in?"

"Couldn't be better." I smiled, then shifted in my seat. "Well, it would be better if we weren't only in the beginning stages of upgrading my old place. Ethan wants to use it as a rental."

"That's a fantastic idea!"

"That's what I thought as well. This experience,

working together on that project, is also giving us time to work on our relationship and strengthen it." I giggled.

"I bet it is. Renovations aren't easy. I'll tell you if you can navigate that, you two will be fine. Look at Thomas and I."

It was true; they had survived the expansion of Bluebird Books, and now they were adding an addition to Thomas's workshop.

"True."

"Still mad at me for making you take part in that program?"

I laughed to myself as Melinda stepped up to take our order. "Morning, ladies."

"Morning, Melinda." I smiled. "Your father says hello."

"How's the old man doing today?"

I couldn't help but laugh. Ethan hated when she called him an old man. "He was heading over to help Thomas at the shop this morning when I left."

"Yes, he told me he was going to help there. It will be good for him. Will you two be having the usual?"

Trinity and I both nodded and watched as Melinda made her way over to another table that had just come in.

I looked over at my best friend. Her heart had been in the right place. It just didn't feel like it was at the beginning. I smiled. "I'm not mad. Honestly, I think it was the best decision you ever made, putting my letter in that box."

"I'm glad."

I looked up in time to see Brooke come out of the kitchen, her eyes red from what appeared to be crying. She whispered something to Melinda and Cici, wringing her hands together as she spoke. Each one of them wiping their eyes as she continued to speak.

"What is going on over there?" I whispered, making Trinity turn around and look over her shoulder.

"Whatever it is, it doesn't appear to be good," Trinity replied.

I glanced out the window and saw both Thomas and Ethan heading to the door of The Crispy Biscuit, both with concerned looks on their faces. Thomas came in first, glancing around for us, and once they found us, they came over to the table.

"What's going on?" I asked, looking up at Ethan, who signaled for me to slide over, Thomas doing the same.

"Would you two please tell us what is going on?"

"We were out at Gabe's to deliver the blanket boxes he ordered. He looked upset, so of course we asked. It's Harry. He's suffered a fall. Bessy had to close the inn."

I looked over at Trinity and wrapped my arm through Ethan's as tears filled my eyes.

"What?" I choked out, my throat tight with emotion at the thought of poor Harry and Bessy having to close the only thing they'd ever known. "Do you know anything else?"

Thomas shook his head. "Gabe didn't know."

I slid my hand into Ethan's as he wrapped his arm around me and placed a kiss on my forehead.

Tristan and Brooke soon joined us at our table, with us making room for the two of them to sit down. The rest of the morning, the three of us sat together, eating sweets and drinking coffee while a heavy, dark feeling fell over the town.

Ethan was already asleep when I slipped into bed. I lay beside him, reading the latest romance book from my favorite author, and let out a yawn. It had been a long day. We'd gotten two rooms painted at my old place and a pile of boxes unpacked tonight.

I placed the book down on the nightstand and removed my reading glasses, reaching up and shutting off the light. Morning would come early. I had a busy day ahead of me at the shop, and Ethan was once again helping Thomas at his shop. We also still had some unpacking to do. Regardless of the work ahead of us, I finally felt content. I snuggled down under the covers and rolled onto my side. Ethan slipped his arm under my head, the other around my waist, and placed a kiss on the side of my neck.

"Love you," he whispered.

"Love you too." I snuggled back into him, letting the warmth of his body consume me.

I closed my eyes and lay there, thinking about our future. The possibilities we had in front of us were exciting to think about and something to look forward to.

I never imagined being able to say good-bye to Darren. Holding onto him seemed the right thing to do when consumed with guilt that his accident had been my fault. However, forgiving myself had turned out to be the better option.

I had Ethan to thank for that. His words, his kindness, his persistence, and that he felt the same way when Polly had passed made it easier, even though it didn't seem like that. What started out as something I didn't want to do, a few exchanged letters with a stranger, turned out to be the best thing that ever happened to me. After all, it was all the letters from our hearts and time spent together that allowed me to forgive myself, heal, and learn to love again.

Next in the Willow Valley Series is Connor and Cadence's story in What Once Was Broken.

There was a whole pile of reasons I didn't want to return to Willow Valley. Small town, everyone knows everyone's business, I'd have to face the man who broke my heart by marrying my best friend, and the fact that she is now gone. Yet somehow I'm convinced to go.

Find out what happens in this return to hometown, older brother's best friend, second chance romance.

Available Now

Follow S.L. Sterling

Did you know that bookbub has a feature where you can follow me and it will send you an alert when I release a book or put a title on sale? Sign up here and make sure you stay in the loop.

Bookbub:
https://geni.us/SLSterlingBookbub

Website
https://www.authorslsterling.com

Facebook
https://geni.us/SLSterlingFB

Twitter
https://geni.us/SLSterlingTwitter

Instagram
https://geni.us/SLSterlingInstagram

Tiktok
https://geni.us/slsterlingtiktok

Reader Group

https://geni.us/SapphiresReaderGroup

Goodreads
https://geni.us/SterlingGoodreads

Newsletter
https://geni.us/NLSignupBackMatter

About the Author

USA Today Bestselling Author S.L. Sterling was born and raised in southern Ontario. She now lives in Northern Ontario Canada and is married to her best friend and soul mate and their two dogs.

An avid reader all her life, S.L. Sterling dreamt of becoming an author. She decided to give writing a try after one of her favorite authors launched a course on how to write your novel. This course gave her the push she needed to put pen to paper and her debut novel "It Was Always You" was born.

When S.L. Sterling isn't writing or plotting her next novel she can be found curled up with a cup of coffee, blanket and the newest romance novel from one of her favorite authors.

In her spare time, she enjoys camping, hiking, sunny destinations, spending quality time with family and friends and of course reading.

To be notified of new releases or sales, join S.L. Sterling's private Mailing List.
https://geni.us/NLSignupBackMatter

Get even more of the inside scoop when you join S.L. Sterling's private Facebook group, Sterling's Silver Sapphires: https://geni.us/SapphiresReaderGroup

Other Titles by S.L. Sterling

It Was Always You

On A Silent Night

Bad Company

Back to You this Christmas

Fireside Love

Holiday Wishes

Saviour Boy

The Boy Under the Gazebo

The Greatest Gift

Into the Sunset

Letting You Go

The Spencer Brooks Diaries

Our Little Secret

Our Little Surprise

Our Little Wedding

The Malone Brother Series

A Kiss Beneath the Stars

In Your Arms

His to Hold

Finding Forever with You

Vegas MMA

Dagger

Doctors of Eastport General

Doctor Desire

Doctor Right

All I Want for Christmas (Contemporary Romance Holiday Collection)

Willow Valley

Memories of the Past

To Trust my Heart

Letters from the Heart

What Once Was Broken

Scars on my Heart

The Happy Holidates Series

Pop Tarts and Mistletoe

Champagne and Fireworks

Summer Nights and Fireflies

Vancouver Dominators

Inside the Penalty Box

Ten Minute Misconduct

www.ingramcontent.com/pod-product-compliance
Lightning Source LLC
Chambersburg PA
CBHW061621190726
48288CB00007B/2417